Wild Horse

Eric Neuenfeldt

Wild Horse

STORIES

UNIVERSITY OF MASSACHUSETTS PRESS
Amherst and Boston

This book is the winner of the 2015 Grace Paley Prize in Short Fiction. The Association of Writers & Writing Programs, which sponsors the award, is a national nonprofit organization dedicated to serving American letters, writers, and programs of writing. Its headquarters are at George Mason University, Fairfax, Virginia, and its website is www.awpwriter.org.

ISBN 978-1-62534-236-2

Designed by Sally Nichols
Set in Adobe Minion Pro
Printed and bound by Sheridan Books, Inc.,

Jacket design by Sally Nichols
Jacket art: Detail of the "Wild Horse" from the Vogelherd Cave,
one of the oldest works of art. The sculpture is in the
Museum Schloss Hohentübingen, Tübingen, Germany.
(Wikimedia Commons CC-BY-SA-4.0)

Library of Congress Cataloging-in-Publication Data

Names: Neuenfeldt, Eric, author.
Title: Wild horse : stories / by Eric Neuenfeldt.
Description: Amherst : University of Massachusetts Press, 2016.
Identifiers: LCCN 2016026497 | ISBN 9781625342362 (jacketed cloth : alk.
paper)
Classification: LCC PS3614.E536 A6 2016 | DDC 813/.6—dc23
LC record available at https://lccn.loc.gov/2016026497

British Library Cataloguing-in-Publication Data
A catalog record for this book is available from the British Library.

For my family

CONTENTS

Wild Horse

Gar

ack Schott's crew is hauling out the heavy-duty saws, the twenty-eight-inch saws, to take down the willow that killed the Islandale kid. The kid's parents have parked their Beemer at the end of the private causeway out to Islandale, rich bastard's island. It took ten thousand wagonloads of Waukesha County gravel to build that causeway and form Muck Bay, my bay, and they probably don't even know it. They stand near the willow directing Mack, showing him that they want the tree to fall into the water, but he brushes them off because he doesn't take bullshit from anyone, rich or not. The willow's not their tree anyway—it belongs to the fat family in the last house, a one-bedroom dump like ours, on the shoreline before the narrow causeway. The fat family's boy paces circles at a safe distance from the tree as one of Mack's crewman cuts down the frayed rope of the tire swing. The bead-stripped Firestone lands in the lake with a quiet slap and the kid jumps in to retrieve the relic before it's lost to the muck.

My cousin Terry hooked a gar underneath that willow once, but the nylon line snapped and the damn thing glided away in triumph, hook in mouth, towing the line and sinkers. Terry watched the small wake until it calmed, then handed me the fishing pole. He stopped fishing after that, avoided the lake altogether, and instead paid attention in school and grew doughy and ended up overweight and in law school at the U of Chicago. And I haven't seen a gar in Muck Bay, townie bay, since.

Across the lawns, Mack gives me a wave. "Hey there," he calls. I look away like I don't notice. He knows Monday I start on his crew and that he'll pretty much have me as a treeman forever. I reach down into the muck and fetch another limestone tumbled away from shore, drawing out lumps of thick mud as I take it up. Pop always used to talk about pouring one of those fancy concrete walls after the city dredged our bay, but we both knew the city would never spend the money. Not here. City Hall will let our bay fill with muck or Pop'll sell first. After Dad passed, Pop said we'd use the money from Dad's tree farm up North, which is also crap because only a fool would buy two acres of needlecast firs. Everyone up North says the farm is cursed now anyway with what happened to Dad last winter. They told us he'd started with scotch after he saw the rows of needle-bare trees, then climbed back into his truck and headed down Highway Q, driving through the snowstorm knowing he had nothing, driving through nowhere, Wisconsin, driving into oblivion.

The door hinge creaks and Pop steps out onto the stoop. He lets the door go and it cracks against the frame. I scoop up a soda can floated into shore. Pop will want to right me after seeing me snub Mack. He'll say something like, "He's your last chance at work, Champ," or some be-lucky-you-have-a-damn-job line. Pop limps across the lawn bow-legged and knees beat from crawling around the concrete floor of someone else's body shop his whole life. "Mack!" he shouts. Mack shouts something back, but his crew has already fired up the pole saw to delimb the tree. The two old bastards shout at each other until I rifle a can at Pop's feet to quiet him. He gives me that old Krauthead frown and crushes the can on his way to shore.

"Shoreline's fucked from the winter freeze," I say.

Pop looks at the pile of slimy limestone. "Don't see why you're bothering. Pier's not going in this year."

"The hell it isn't," I say. Dad's five sections of aluminum pier, the last thing he bought, lean against the house, still shrink-wrapped in blue plastic. "We're the only ones in Muck Bay with an aluminum pier. It's going in."

Pop sighs and eases himself onto the lake-beaten fishing bench Dad built me when I was kid. Fishing brought us, him, back to the lake after Mom dove in beyond the sandbar and went under. Dad never bought another boat.

"Say there, Champ. I was thinking maybe it's time we put your Dad's place up for sale. With you staying in the fish house now and all."

I straighten my back and my weight sinks me knee deep into the muck. Dad's house, the house he built for Mom and him after they married, the only house I know and ever will, sits twenty yards down the shore, shaded by a row of birches, blinds drawn and all sealed up. Beyond Dad's house, Mack's crew works their chainsaws. Pop needs the money. I dip my arms into the murky water and the muck thins and runs off. "We'd lose lake access," I finally say.

"We could work it out with the new owner." Pop coughs when I go back into the muck for another limestone. "Spring's the best time to sell anyway."

"Look, Lefty. You know damn well those developers—"

"Watch your mouth now," he says, turning.

I let out a laugh and pull myself out of the muck and onto shore. I'll call him Lefty, his old shop name at Lake County Auto Service, when I want to disrespect him, to remind him what a weak old man he has become. Our family's been on this property since the city dredged the lake, townies through it all, and I'll go bankrupt before I cave to one of those Chicago suits always coming around.

Pop puts his hands on the bench to support himself. "You know my reasons. Stop horseshitting around. It's time."

"I'm not broke yet," I say. "Mack's putting me on his railroad crew first thing. Double time. Eighteen an hour, cash."

"Clearing brush off the rails ain't no living." Pop winces when he says it, knowing the body shop, his work, isn't too far above cutting down trees for millionaires and their railroads. We should take what we're given. Pop told me that.

"Well," I say after a minute. I clean up with a bucket of hose water. "It's good enough for now."

"If you say." He tries to cover up his sigh with a long yawn. "Terry phoned."

"So."

"He's coming up for a visit later today. Said he'd like to take you to Blondie's for a meal."

"And I'm sure you had nothing to do with that. He bringing that mean bride of his?" I tip the bucket with my foot and let the water flow out into the lawn.

"Don't you talk about Kayla that way. She's good to him."

"She'll split if he doesn't make it."

"Well, maybe he can talk some sense—" But he stops, I stop, when we hear the driveway's gravel popping.

———

Terry doesn't visit Pop much, but when he does, he's always sure to dress in a neatly pressed Oxford and bring all sorts of crap to show how successful he's going to be. Today he's in a white Oxford tucked into linen pants and has a tan that's unapologetically fake—his skin has an orange hue, like he's glazed himself with some kind of marmalade. It's spring and the sun just today has broken through the cloud cover. I hack off a slice of venison sausage with my Dad's dull lockback as Terry unloads his bag of nonsense.

"Yeah, here's something great I found in Chicago." He sets a six-pack of amber bottles onto Pop's kitchen table. "It's a microbrew from Wyoming. You can only get it one place east of the Mississippi, and that place is a liquor store right in Lincoln Park. I'm telling you, you can find things in Chicago you just can't get around here. Not even in Milwaukee. Hope it's still cold." He uncaps three bottles with his key chain opener and hands one to Pop. He holds one out to me. "You up for one, underage?"

I drop the knife and venison and reach for the bottle. The label's started to peel from the bottle sweat and I'm sure the beer's lukewarm. I don't thank him.

"Say, guys. Cheers." He clinks bottles with Pop, but knows better than to try with me.

Pop lets out an uneasy laugh because he knows this family-visit business is bullshit. He tips the bottle and goes teary eyed when he swallows, which means the beer's either car-heated or crap. I start to take a sip myself, but tip the bottle back when the skunk hits my mouth. I would have settled for a can of good ol' Pabst, the only beer made by people who actually drink.

"So what do you guys think?" Terry asks.

"Moose piss," I say and put the bottle back in front of him, label out.

He looks at the leafy logo on the label and smiles. "Well, anyway," he says. "It's what everyone is drinking in Chicago right now."

"Sure," I say, not doubting him. I open my knife back up. I'll kill the taste with venison and chew loud through his bullshit explanation.

Terry reaches back into the bag. "Say, Pop, got you some cheese at the state line. Couldn't help myself. Not too often that I get back up here." He unloads three bricks of cheese, which Pop about knocks over his bottle to snatch.

"Hand me the knife there, Champ," he says to me. I set down the lockback and find him a knife in the drawer.

As Pop digs into the cheese, I start to wonder if the beer was from the state line too, some garbage that Terry'd never heard of, so he thought he could palm it off like some grand discovery. What a load. Before I can call him out, he starts up again. "I heard about the Islandale kid down in Chicago," he says.

"No shit," Pop says, digging through Terry's grocery bag to see what else he's brought.

"Yeah, he was an undergraduate at Chicago. From a wealthy family. Real sad. The article said he'd been drinking some."

"Some?" I say. "He was trashed. He threw this big party out there, got sauced, decided to jump the little bridge on the causeway, and slammed into a tree. So much for the vacation house. You should have seen the car. Of course now his folks have to cut down the fat family's willow."

Terry chokes down a swallow of his beer. "Well, people make poor decisions sometimes." He tries giving me a hard stare, but he's almost a lawyer now, so just looks like an ass. If I knew he wouldn't press charges, I'd send him home with a shiner.

"Terry, why you got night crawlers in the bag?" Pop tries to settle us. He opens the top of the Styrofoam container and drags his thumb though the slimy dirt and newspaper.

"I saw those worms in the store on the state line and couldn't resist. Thought I'd give fishing another try after we talked. Maybe you'll take me, Champ," he says, looking at me. He calls me Champ, my nickname since I was a kid, like Pop, to tell me I'm immature, to say I haven't gone anywhere because I didn't up and go to college.

Pop nods. "Sounds better than lunch at Blondie's. The food's gone to shit since you were here last, honestly. New owners. You boys catch something other than a carp and I'll clean it and fry it up."

"That'd be great, Pop," Terry says. He starts over to the counter and taps my arm as he passes. "Say, Champ, why don't you gather up some fishing poles while I talk to Pop about a few things."

"Shit. Fine, fine," I say. I turn to the counter. Terry goes after the venison, but I brush away his hand and grab the lockback before he can get a good handle on it.

———

Pop sits at the kitchen table buying Terry's line. I struggle with the rust-seized Master Lock on the shed behind the house, but it's no use. Terry'll convince Pop to let him sell the place for a share, and Pop will trust him. Terry unloaded his mom's place in town for a song and paid for four years of Marquette with his cut. It'll be a big cut, and Pop and I will be on our ass. I head for the fish house where I keep my good rod and reel. Terry isn't here to fish anyway.

Mack's crew has taken the tree down to its trunk and they all stand around and drink from paper cups and flip coins to decide who'll man the twenty-eight-inch saw. If I were on the crew now, they'd show me how to work the saw, their saw, then have me do it, laughing as splinters of tree kick up into my face. But I'll know better. Dad taught me how to use a saw up North and I'll be ready. I'll fell a tree onto their truck if they give me any shit. I'm that good.

I stand behind the fish house and peer inside Pop's kitchen window. Pop is picking at the buttons of his flannel, which means he's already given in. I know he thinks I'm close to breaking down. I was the only one around when that Islandale kid ran his Explorer into that willow. Pop had gone to Lake County Auto to work some hours since I'd hauled off and belted my boss at a pizza joint in town. The job was lousy—heating frozen pizzas in a commercial-sized microwave oven, and I'd rather bum around the yard clearing gutters and replacing rotten boards on Pop's house. Pop didn't say anything about that one either. He knows it wasn't a real job anyway.

I didn't want to go over to help the kid, but the 911 lady said it was my *civic duty* to stand there and keep the kid talking until the ambulance showed to haul his battered ass down to Memorial. *Civic duty.* That's how they talk around here. The front end of his Explorer was pushed into accordion folds back to the windshield and I knew the kid'd be a mess. The engine hissed and exhaled little breaths of ruin. The radio played southern rock, some real studio shit that nobody outside Nashville, nobody around here, would ever listen to. I saw the blood first. *Hey, buddy. They're on their way.* The red taillights blinked steadily. They'd told us a farmer found Dad when he saw the taillights in a row of pines deep off the roadside. *Hey, buddy. Any chance you can turn off the damn lights?* The air bag filled the front windshield of the Explorer. Dad's heaper didn't have an air bag. I went around to the passenger side and found the seatbelt retracted and the kid's head inside the dash's center panel. I asked for a picture of Dad's steering wheel, but Pop said it wouldn't make any difference. *Hey, buddy. Can you hear the sirens coming?* I couldn't manage an image. The willow will burn fast as our firewood this winter. Pop reaches across his kitchen table and gives Terry a firm handshake. *Hey, buddy, they're here. And they're going to take good care of you now.*

———

Terry insists on driving, but to hell with that, the fishing spot is only four hundred yards down the road. He's already developed that aristocrat waddle—his ankles are swollen and rolling out from all the study-snack weight, from spending the week pinched in stiff dress shoes. He stays quiet and squeezes into the Honda hybrid he just leased. If Pop weren't so desperate, he'd have thrown Terry out for not buying American. The old Pop, the broken-kneed Pop, the heat-dizzy after working a double shift Pop, would have told Terry to get the hell out of his home, that no grandkid of his would ever drive around in anything but a American-blooded GM product. Come back, he'd say, when you're driving a car with some U.S. steel around you.

When I pass the narrow driveway out to Islandale, I try to wave to Mack, try to make up for brushing him off earlier, but he's tied up with the Islandale folks and I want no part of that, not yet anyway.

Terry pulls up alongside me and rolls down his window. "Hey, Champ, where can I park?"

I keep on walking, but he coasts with me. "That's why you shouldn't have driven. You'll have to park on the shoulder and hope a semi doesn't swipe your car," I say.

Terry purses his lips and speeds off. I hope he's forgotten where the break in the tree line is that opens up to the trail down to the creek that feeds Muck Bay. I hope he keeps driving. He could drive clear to Madison and it wouldn't be far enough for me.

Beyond the small bridge, just beyond the trail's entrance, Terry signals and pulls onto the shoulder and glides his car into the roadside's canary grass. Some people in town spend lifetimes trying to keep their families together, to stay tethered to one another. I spend the afternoon trying to getting rid of mine. I kick the shoulder's gravel to pelt his back bumper, but I don't have the same kick. As a kid, I'd kick stones at Terry's legs the entire way to the trail, and by summer's end he'd have whole constellations of nicks and scabs on his calves.

"Saw that," he says, slamming his door. "It's time you grow up, Champ."

"I missed," I say. I consider running the fishing pole's tip along the car door, but that'd be too much, not in front of him anyway.

"You know I can't be coming up here every time Pop needs something. You're twenty now. Take some responsibility."

I let him go, the only way to stop him, and start down the short trail to the creek. He'll lecture me all the way to the creek and we'll end up with nothing if I don't shut my trap. The ice has gone out and we're here just before the spawn. It's peak walleye season, when they're migrating to the sandy feeder creeks to spawn. Pop used to send Terry and me down here after school with a basket to fill for dinner and we'd fish until sundown. Terry had a spinning reel and carbon rod his mom bought him after his old man split and would fish with a spoon. He'd cast and reel the lure out and in as if challenging the walleye to chase the flash. I didn't mind touching the worms and used the jointed bamboo poles Pop gave Terry and me before we could walk—a tie-on line with a hook and a bobber. I'd roll up my blue jeans like goddamn Huck Finn and hop on the Indian rocks, working the two poles until the basket was full and then I'd make Terry haul the basket back to Pop. But Terry'd always tell Pop and Dad that he'd caught them all, every last one. And they always let him because they knew bullshit was all he had.

"Here," I say, handing him the fishing rod. "Get a worm on that hook."

Terry takes the rod and flicks a practice cast, as if it matters. "You couldn't have brought two?"

"You're the one that wanted to fish." I jump the four-foot gap from the shore to the first Indian rock. There've been hundreds of feet on these rocks, the rocks the Indians set, and every rock has held steady while the fisher caught his take.

"The worms are slimy," Terry says. He prods the dirt of the Styrofoam container.

"Just shut up and fish already. You're scaring away the damn fish." Two walleye wave their tails a few times and slink away. We're well ahead of the spawn.

Terry stabs the hook through the worm once, then wraps the worm around the hook's bend—the lazy way. He reaches down and splashes his hand through the water. "The water is still cold."

I take the flask from my back pocket and uncap it. "Just fish," I say. I take a sip. Cool whiskey. Sipping whiskey. Dad taught me how to drink down by this creek and everything always goes smoother when I'm standing on the Indian rocks as the spring current flows past me and feeds Muck Bay, my bay again.

"What's in the flask?" Terry asks. He leans in for a closer look at the worm, probably to see if the worm'll stay. I know he'll lose it on one cast.

"Something to burn off that bullshit beer you bought us."

Terry snorts. "You're a sconnie and always will be."

I take another sip, let the slight burn rest on my tongue. "Damn straight."

A gar glides in the gap between the rocks beside me. I stand still so I don't spook it. I've been fishing this creek all my life and rarely see them, not since Terry's line broke anyway. The gar moves through the clear water like it knows it's ancient and changeless and uncatchable.

"Gar," Terry whispers. He takes a step and dips his shoe's toe into the water, then backs off. Terry releases the bail and winds up to cast.

"Don't you do it," I say.

"Relax. It's a gar. It's legal."

"To hell it is."

Terry eases up and pulls a pamphlet out of his back pocket. "I stopped and bought a license on my way up. Read the rules too. They're rough fish. Totally legal." He casts the line beyond the gar and lets the bait settle into the shallow water.

"Don't test me," I say, but Terry doesn't hear. Mack's crew starts up the twenty-eight-inch saws and readies to take down the willow's trunk. Terry cranks the reel, positions the bait in front of the gar's nose. I feel for Dad's lockback in my pocket and flip open the blade. It took the firemen two hours to cut Dad out of his truck's twisted steel after the accident. Live bait. The gar takes it. Terry lets the fish hook before he reels. I won't let Pop sell. The chain saw hits the willow, doesn't kick back, and the crewman begins through the wood's rings. I set my foot on the rock's flat part. Terry reels and brings the line taut as I lunge for blue nylon, but my foot lets go. And even underneath, where the gar struggles its stay, I can hear the saw blade traveling through the center.

Temper

I was tied up with a brake-bleed when Grandma Jo barged into the shop and told me my aunt Gloria had finally offed herself. Gloria voluntarily committed herself to the loony bin out in 'Tosa often, so Grandma Jo said I should have been expecting it. True, for as long as I could remember, Gloria hauled around a big purse with several orange bottles of pills rattling around inside. Whenever she talked to someone longer than a minute or two, she would have to pop a handful of pills just to finish the conversation. She also liked to disappear and would turn up broke and confused in bus stations in inner-city Detroit and Cleveland. Her death gave us a new concern, though: my cousin Jeep would be coming back into town.

"She hanged herself with the bed sheets," Grandma Jo said. "I bet everyone in the ward thought the ceiling couldn't support her weight. Old building. Spanish plaster. To think of her hanging there." She watched me pump brake fluid into the line and probably considered critiquing my work even though she didn't know a damn thing about bikes. She always had to assert herself as the alpha and insult a man's work, even if it was worth a compliment. "Well, if that's what Gloria wanted," she said after a while. She took a matchbook off the workbench and lit a Virginia Slim.

Landry, the shop owner, a jittery ex-cokehead who paid us cash under the table and didn't believe in things like safety guards on power tools, stomped down the stairs. "Lady, lady," he said. "You can't smoke in my shop. Get the hell out of here with that thing." Grandma Jo ashed into a grease tub. She smoked two packs a day and lit up freely indoors, not really giving a shit about health because her doctor had sentenced her to death: emphysema. She gave my boss a casual glance and turned back to me. "I've never cared for the bald. Especially the bald and short. It's no surprise this shop is such a dump."

"Easy, Grandma," I said. I was going through a polite phase because I was on my second rotation through all the shops in the city and no one really wanted me anymore. A month before I had interviewed for a gig testing tempers, the life of metals, at a steel plant, but they hadn't called me and never would.

But Grandma Jo was right: Landry kept a filthy shop. There were piles of orphaned parts everywhere—derailleurs he'd poached pulleys from, hub bodies he'd disemboweled. He thought chores like cleaning were a waste of employee time, and he sure as hell wasn't going to sweep, mop, or dust himself. Most shop owners I'd worked for would hire some kid from one of the shady neighborhoods to scrub the toilet and floors after school—that's how everyone in the bike biz gets their start—but not Landry. The solution circulator on our parts washer had been busted since spring, and he just told us to deal and clean parts in the murky degreaser.

"Just get her out of here, jackass," Landry said.

I took Grandma Jo's cigarette and put it out on my workbench and led her into the alley. The skinhead who ran the garage across the alley was taking a break from fitting a muffler so he could empty his scrap metal into our shop's Dumpster. His face was inked with deep blue hate. As he dragged a rusted-out exhaust pipe past us, Grandma Jo said, "That's some face you got there, son."

The guy paused a moment. "Excuse me?" he said.

"Oh, don't even bother," she said. "The damage has been done." Grandma Jo ran my grandfather's auto body shop for twenty years after he died and had a solid handle on his type, so she wasn't about to take any bullshit from him. Hell, she'd probably rejected his application at one point. "Go on back over to your side of the alley," she said to him. He heaved the pipe into our Dumpster and retreated.

"I don't know why you insist on working in this god-awful neighborhood. With people like that around. You're going to get yourself killed."

"I like it here," I said, which was the truth. Landry rented me the tiny studio apartment above the shop, where I had a single-burner stove and a mini-fridge, so I didn't have a commute. The only trouble I had was when the guy at the garage worked late and his friends and him would rifle empty bottles of Budweiser at my lit window. Nights I saw them roll in, I would turn off all the lights and sit still until the sounds of death-metal and power pipe cutters died down, which was about five in the morning.

"Well, any time you want to learn a real trade." Grandma Jo licked her fingertips, yellowed from years of cigarette tar, and cleared what was probably a streak of shop grease from my face. "But we have more pressing matters. Your cousin is on his way back from Ohio."

"Phenomenal," I said. My cousin Jeep had inherited the pill problem from my aunt. He fled Milwaukee at sixteen and had spent the better part of a decade trying on selves in the Plains and Rockies. At one point he changed his name to Chance Story and started a cult in the Four Corners. Ten or so other psychos joined, and they started growing what he called industrial hemp, but they all ended up spending a few years in the slammer for cultivating primo bud. Last I'd heard he was working in a medical sharps factory in an off-the-map town in Ohio, probably the right kind of job for someone with a felony drug conviction.

"You'll need to fetch him from the Greyhound station tomorrow," Grandma Jo said. "He's wanting a ride to her apartment to gather some of her things."

"Why the hell would I do that? All she owned was garbage," I said. "Literal garbage, Grandma."

"Watch that mouth of yours," she said. She hooked her hand around my collar and gave me a shake like she used to when I was a pup.

But Gloria did own nothing but garbage. She lived in a subsidized one-bedroom near the fenced-in lot where Dahmer's old torture chamber once stood. He lived in Oxford Apartments Number Three, and I'm sure she was in Number Five. Inside she had a bed, the mattress appropriated from a Marquette kid's broken futon, and piles of garbage that she'd gathered out of the trash barrels in front of Judy's Red Hots and Wendy's. Styrofoam cups with melted ice and Pepsi, the nubs of discarded hot dogs. I tried to give her a microwave one time, but she just shoved a bunch of garbage in there and started a fire. The next day she took the bus down to my apartment, knocked on my door, and dropped the microwave on my feet when I answered. The thing filled her head with soft voices, she said.

Grandma Jo stopped shaking me, and I apologized. "Things have been rough here at work," I said.

"Oh, Christ. Won't you toughen up already?" She lit another Virginia Slim and tossed the match in my direction.

"Fine. Yeah, I'll take care of it."

"There's also the issue of the funeral."

"Funeral?" I asked. "I'm not going to a funeral. That would require me to wear a suit." My extended family, an enormous German farm family with thirty-seven second cousins, people who still clung to things like deer hunting and Lutheranism, lived west of Milwaukee and up North. I would periodically receive a phone call about a funeral for some vague relative who'd keeled over. Those of us who ventured into the city to live couldn't waste time and money—we didn't have much of either—on going back for all these funerals. My grandparents were the first generation to abandon the country and they passed down to me the attitude of never returning. Grandma Jo said I would be incinerated if I died before her. She said I shouldn't expect much after death.

"It's not quite a funeral," Grandma Jo said. "More of a barn party. Tomorrow night. At Donny Kappel's farm. He's calling it a celebration of life."

"I hope you declined for all of us." Donny Kappel was my second or third cousin, twice or three times removed—who the hell even bothered to track this stuff anymore?—and would meddle in our affairs every now and then because he lived an hour away, the closest relative, geographically speaking. By all reports he was a lousy farmer, so just contracted his fields to commercial agriculture companies run by people who understood things like crop cycles and weather patterns.

The skinhead guy emerged from the inner circle of his garage office with a grinding wheel. He plugged it in, tested the motor, and started grinding what looked like a new-used section of exhaust. He angled the blade against metal, sending a spray of spark into the alley where we were standing.

"This guy," Grandma Jo said. She took a few more drags off her Virginia Slim and walked over to the garage and extinguished the cigarette on the garage's lit sign. This burned a small hole in the plastic so that a pinhole of yellow light shone through the red, something to remember her by.

She turned back to me. She didn't need to say anything more because I already knew I'd fire up my Oldsmobile 88 the next day and drive that lunatic around and hope he didn't steal my car. "Two o'clock tomorrow," she said. "Don't run away or whatever it is you do when you decide to disappear. Time a man in this family stopped dodging real trouble."

———

A smear of dried blood ran across one of the glass panels on the revolving doors into the Greyhound station. I pulled my sleeve over my hand and pushed through the doors. Inside the lobby, an elderly janitor wearing a Dickies one-piece used a broom as a cane as he moved across the lobby. He stopped to let me clear out of his path.

"I think there's blood on the door," I said, in case he hadn't seen it already. By the looks of the window though, it seemed like someone had taken one square in the gut and backed the exit wound right into the glass.

"That?" he said, looking toward the door. "That's been there for a while." He shuffled off across the lobby.

Jeep was draped over a bench, ratty camo jacket pulled over his face. I walked up and gave him a kick. He pulled the jacket down, squinted at me, and put the jacket back over his face.

"You of all people," he said through the jacket. "I didn't think Grandma Jo would send you. Fuck off."

I could have left him right there, stuck to that bench gooey with chewing gum and spilled Mountain Dew. I had reason. Before he skipped town ten years before, he jumped me while I was pedaling out to the Schwinn shop so I could bleach toilets for minimum wage. He rolled up in some burnout's station wagon, five deep in the back. The wagon ran me off the road and he jumped out and tackled me. He had a two-by-four. He pressed the rough-cut edge against my head and whispered, "I want to remake your temple for what you've done." Of course, I hadn't done shit—he was just a lunatic who wanted my bike to pawn. The money from that bike was enough to help him get out of town. That was the last time I'd seen the jerk.

I grabbed a handful of the coat, the patch right over his face, and tore it off. He had a broad scar that ran the length of the crease of his forehead that I didn't remember being there before. His beard was long, Ted Kaczynski–style, and climbed up high on his cheekbones.

"You have me as a driver for one day thanks to Grandma Jo," I said. I went to fold his coat and a switchblade and a bottle of pills with the label torn off fell out of it. I picked them up, tossed the pills into his lap, and dumped the knife in a trashcan.

"You need to decide whether or not you're going to fuck this up," I said.

He popped the cap on the pills with one hand and pitched a few into his mouth. "I'm not the one who should be worried," he said.

As he closed the bottle's lid, I caught the mangled stump that was his left hand sticking out from his sweater's sleeve. I'd almost forgotten about the stump, the hand he'd all but blown off after he lit the body of an M80 one Fourth of July. We were standing on the diving platform in the middle of the pond on Donny Kappel's farm, and Jeep was lighting M80s and throwing them into the water. Grandma Jo had deposited all the truly old folks in lawn chairs down by the shore so they could watch the water rise after each explosion. Jeep was sparking the wicks with a wand lighter, not really paying attention until he lit the body of one and it blew apart his hand. The blast sent bits of bone and gristle all over me. Old people screamed. Lawn chairs toppled. And there Jeep was in the water, splashing around in a cloud of red, trying to hold the stump above the waterline as he paddled to shore. No one could help him, not for a long time, not ever.

"All right, bitch," Jeep finally said. He punched me with his stump. "I'll take that ride to my ma's crib. There's some business I have to see to."

We left the station and climbed into my car and drove through the Valley toward his mother's old building. We passed the gravel distributor, the remnants of the Falk factory that had exploded the previous winter, chemical plants pumping byproduct into the sky.

Jeep cranked down the window, which slipped off the track at a certain point and just fell into the door. "Brew City, U.S.A.," he said. "Asshole of America."

"Better than Ohio." I turned and picked up the Sixteenth Street Bridge over the freeway and into the brief glam of Marquette. A college kid darted out between two buildings into the street, but I didn't slow for him. The school had dropped me after a semester on scholarship.

"I would have hit him," Jeep said. He turned the dial on the radio with his good hand, but the radio had always been burned out. He tried the knob again and again before finally yanking it off the radio and launching it out the window. "Don't even have a fucking radio. I see you haven't made much progress since I've been gone. Don't think this means I'm going to talk to you now."

I considered letting him have it, but we were on the street of Gloria's building. We coasted past the lot to Dahmer's old building and I pulled over to the curb. Before I could even throw the 88 into park, Jeep was out of the car and headed up the steps to the building's door. The buzzer never worked so you could just head right in. I didn't know why he was racing up to her apartment because I had a key for the place that Grandma Jo had given me. Turns out he didn't need it. By the time I got up to the apartment, he had already pushed in the cheesy door, tore the deadbolt straight out of the doorframe.

"Place has already been ransacked," Jeep said. The place looked like someone had done some snooping, sure, but Jeep ignored the feathers and splatters of white and purple bird shit on the floor. Apparently a number of birds had made their nest inside the apartment while Aunt Gloria was off having her final meltdown. He shooed one of the offenders and the thing flew out of the broken window.

Jeep pulled the futon mattress flat and tore the sheet off. He found a seam and worked his good hand in and broke the threads the length of the mattress. What he couldn't see was that the other side had already been cut, exposing limp, dirty stuffing, so whatever he was looking for had already been pinched. He rooted around for a bit, then dropped the mattress. "Fucking hell. I bet the landlord got to it before me. No, no, I bet it was Grandma Jo. Always thinking about money, that woman."

"I don't think she's interested in Gloria's money," I said. I used my foot to search through a pile of trash, but gave up when I unearthed what seemed to be a three-month-old chicken sandwich. I set my shirt collar on the bridge of my nose and backed into the doorframe, not that the mold in the walls and carpet out in the hallway made for any better breathing.

Jeep struck the bed's flimsy headboard with his stump and put a healthy dent in it. "Goddamn, I know she's the one who took it. She has my fucking inheritance." He clocked the headboard again and sank to the ground. "Shit, shit, shit." He was breathing heavily and punching his open palm with the stump. "Right there in the mattress. My ma was a smart like that—never trusted the banks."

I should have felt worse for the guy than I did, the money the only thing left over from his mother gone, but something terrible had happened to her and all he could think about was a couple hundred bucks in a shoebox. He probably thought he was in line for a couple grand, that she had stashed away money from some mysterious income source, or he wouldn't have made the trip up.

Jeep stopped panting. He stood, adjusted his sweater, and looked at me. He gave me a cheap, bipolar smile. "Say, is Grandma Jo going to be at that barn party she mentioned?"

"Sure is, but seems like you have to talk to that landlord," I said.

I was trying my best to find a reason to leave him there in the bird's nest, to keep him away from Grandma Jo, but he wasn't having any of it.

"Bullshit," he said. He walked over to the doorframe and examined the damage to the deadbolt like somebody else had caused it. "I'd like to see everyone. And I'm guessing they'd like to see me."

"Only if you don't show up empty-handed," I said.

———

Jeep never much cared for Donny Kappel's lame animals. By lame I don't mean boring, but broken, afflicted in the body. He rescued mistreated and unwanted farm animals from trigger-happy owners and vets. Even though I always thought Donny was a little creepy and lazy—he spent his afternoons listening to the rainforest on tape and practicing what he called visualization therapy—I admired his work with the animals. He had pile of them: a dog with three legs, a llama some asshole tortured with various branding irons, a donkey another jerk whipped and blinded.

The donkey stood in the center of the pen, flapping its tail. We leaned over the plastic split-rail fence Donny had had installed. "That donkey's got some—"

"Oh, please. Don't even say it, Jeep," I said. I backed away from the fence because I figured he'd retaliate for me shutting him down like that. But he didn't say anything, just stood up on the bottom rail and swung back and forth on the fence. The llama, a friendly guy I'd named Fletcher when I was in high school, came trotting over.

"Hi, boy," I said.

"Well if it isn't dumpy and stumpy," Grandma Jo said from behind me. I turned and there she was with a deep plastic glass full of pre-made margarita. "You couldn't have at least changed your shirt since yesterday? You stink like tires and degreaser." She took a swig of the margarita and winced. Fall was setting in and frozen drinks probably weren't the best choice, but Donny refused to serve anything else. He was about the only guy in Wisconsin who didn't serve beer—Leinie's, New Glarus, hell, even Pabst—at his parties.

"You there," she said to Jeep. "You going to say hello to your grandma?"

Jeep didn't say anything. He prodded Fletcher with the two nubs on his stump. Fletcher didn't mind being petted, but tended to freak out if you tried anything else. You couldn't expect these rescues to meet slight aggression with anything but greater aggression. They could sense aggression. They could probably smell it on a human.

Fletcher bit Jeep.

Jeep pulled his hand back and fell off the fence. "Fucker," he said. He picked himself up off the dirt and raised his fist at Fletcher, but stopped when he glanced over and saw Grandma Jo and me moving for him. Fletcher had caught what was left of his index finger.

"Boy, you strike that poor animal and I'll see to it that your good hand meets the same fate as the bad," Grandma Jo said.

Jeep wrapped his bleeding stump in the belly of his sweater. Now I would think Jeep would have encountered a few farm animals in Ohio, but apparently he was too busy filching syringes from the sharps factory. He never was much for the outdoors, which made the whole cultivation bust a little surprising.

"Always struggled with that hand out here," I said to Grandma Jo.

"Enough now," she said. "Your cousin could probably use a drink. We'll go fetch you a drink now, Jeep."

"About time someone around here did something for me," he said.

Grandma Jo and I headed for the barn where Donny was pouring pre-made margaritas out of a slushy machine. In an effort to make a little money, he was planning to open his farm to private groups for hayrides and fall harvest festivities. He'd planted a pumpkin patch. A corn maze was under construction. He brought in a trio of Porta-Potties. And apparently he thought his new business venture required some bar accessories like a margarita maker.

When we reached the barn, Grandma Jo grabbed my arm. "Get him something to drink but don't put any booze in it. You know his temper when he drinks. Just like his father."

"I'm pretty sure he's an alcoholic, grandma. I think he'll notice."

Grandma Jo and I watched Jeep pop open a bottle of pills and take a handful. He threw the bottle into the animal pen and walked across the yard toward the Porta-Potties. "Just make sure he stays away from the booze," Grandma Jo said. "I need to use the restroom. Watch him. Do something for once."

Even though none of us had seen Jeep since he was sixteen, we'd seen him plenty drunk. If you grow up in Wisconsin, chances are adults will let you drink underage around them after a while. Jeep tended to cause a scene when he was drinking, which was pretty much nonstop. His father had been a fierce drunk, a failed engineer who up and moved to Florida to work as a ride operator at Disney World. We all learned later that he had a coronary right there in the park. Jeep had a hard time keeping it together after that.

I looked up and saw Grandma Jo cross Jeep. "I know you took that money," I heard him say.

She paused and turned. "What's that? What are you talking about?"

"The money in the apartment. My inheritance. You stole it."

"I have no idea what you're talking about," she said.

She opened the door and went inside the Porta-Potty. Jeep followed. He marched right up to the thing and started shaking it. He hit it with his shoulder and it rocked. He hit it again and started to push it off its platform. Another shot or two and he would have tipped it. "Goddamn you, woman. Goddamn you."

Someone screamed. People stood and drifted toward the

confrontation. I'd had it. I'm not the violent type, but I took off after him. Far as I could tell, he wasn't family anymore. He was a jackass trying to knock over a Porta-Potty with my grandmother inside.

I grabbed ahold of him and threw him aside, but he recovered easily and popped me in the jaw with his stump. The scar across his forehead was red and puffed up. His sweater was bloodied from the llama bite. A few other distant relatives ran across the yard to join in—everyone wanted a free shot at Jeep. He saw them coming. He ran for one of the tables and snagged a pair of camera bags and took off for the corn maze. We all gave chase. The maze wasn't complete, so he didn't have many places to hide. Beyond that, it was several acres of open field.

I ran along one of the maze's walls. I heard the crunch of foot-steps nearby, then saw Jeep's shadow between the stalks. He settled behind a short stretch of hay bales, and I followed. He unzipped a camera bag and rifled through the contents. I slipped my keys out of my pocket and shook my house key out and wedged it between my middle and ring fingers. Jeep heard me, the clink of the keys against one another, but that wouldn't change what I was about to do. It was the rattle before the strike.

He dropped the camera bag and stood. I waited for him in a narrow gap between two corn stalks. A gust of wind came and the edge of a dried husk scratched my face. Jeep pushed through the stalks and went for me, but his foot slid in the loose soil. I swung. He caught my arm and twisted it, but I didn't let him take me down. I broke free, punched the key into his gut, and unlocked him.

Alley Cat

*T*ruck sent me to some bullshit address down in the industrial intestines of the Valley, damn near the tracks along Pigsville. I spun along a narrow access road near West Canal, along the murky wastewater of the Menomonee, through the lots of gutted tugboats, crippled semi-trailers, and tweaked construction cranes. Even though the city threw a little dough at the Valley to repave the winter-beaten roads, you still didn't want to be out riding around down there at dusk without some kind of plan. Especially if you didn't know where the hell you were, exactly. Sure, I'd hit the taco joint by the Sixth Street Viaduct on my way home from the shop, ridden—always in a pack—through the Valley to go see the Brew Crew when some customer slipped me a free ticket in the nose-bleeds. But, mostly I just rode down to Bayview and picked up Water to the Northside to avoid the Valley altogether.

I had reason for this attitude: Quilt, a pretty mean crit racer and my best customer at the shop, liked riding down in the Valley, said the streets were nice and quiet, but got swiped by a cement truck one night. Quilt was caught up in the wheelwell, and something in the truck's undercarriage tore his leg right off. He said the damn thing was just dangling there by a few strands of tissue and cartilage when the paramedics showed up. The doctors managed to reattach the leg, and he had some foolish number of skin grafts so when he was done his friends ended up calling him Quilt, and so did all the wrenches at the shop. Lame leg and all, dude still rides the Valley every night after work.

Anyway, I slowed and coasted off the side of the road and dug out the flyer with the address for my first checkpoint. Sure enough, the address was bogus. So I pulled out my phone and called Truck to say, What the fuck? But he didn't answer, the bastard.

Across a lot of scrapped washing machines and propane tanks, I saw some grizzly old dude shuffling through piles of rusted engine parts, so I pedaled over to him to see if he knew where the hell I was.

"Howdy," I said when I was close enough. I didn't spook him. I wouldn't have been surprised if the old man had a revolver stashed underneath his sweater.

He was holding a small engine. For a lawn mower or weed whacker, maybe. He looked up. His left eye was clouded over and his face was flecked with scabs. "Ever hear of trespassing, young man?"

I held up my arms like I was about to be robbed, and there was a good chance I was. "I was arrested for it once when I was a kid. They sent me to juvie for ten days."

"Get the hell off my property," the guy said, and tossed the engine onto a pile of scrap. "Before I remove you myself."

I started to turn and bail, but stopped. See, I'd spent my entire childhood dealing with mean old assholes like this guy, guys who thought I was some sort of weirdo for always tinkering with bicycles I'd picked out of Dumpsters around the neighborhood. "Get out of there. That's garbage, kid," they'd say. Hell, I was raised by the lowest of them, an alky electrician who lost his license after he botched a commercial job out in 'Tosa and the building went up during the night. He ended up sorting shredded blue jeans and pitted-out T-shirts at the Goodwill warehouse downtown because they were the only people who felt sorry enough for him to take on someone like that part-time. So I tried not to take shit from the ancient and disgruntled.

Plus, I was tired of Truck's crap, sending me to fake addresses in the shittiest neighborhoods so I'd finish Dead Friggin' Last. The alley cat race prize for being DFL was always a putrid, rain-soaked stuffed animal, carnival-sized, that Truck had plucked from the discard pile behind a church thrift store. After every damn race, the other racers would be stumbling around piss-drunk from all the task checkpoints at slummy taverns and there I'd be like some fucking loony, riding home with one of those puppies, or unicorns or pandas, sticking out of my messenger bag.

I didn't really want to be an alley cat in the first place. My boss paid me overtime to race in the alley cats because he thought it would bring a couple more hipsters into the shop, make it seem like we were down the scene. I wasn't down with the whole deal until my mechanic friend Musky, an older badass who ran a repairs-only shop solo up in the shattered part of West Burleigh, the neighborhood where I grew up, signed on to sponsor a checkpoint. He was trying to drum up some business too. Musky was a surly ex-motorhead turned bike geek, a guy forced into working on bikes by one too many DUIs. None of the shops around town would hire him because he was ancient and fairly senile, so he scraped together enough cash to start his own turd shop. Thing was his shop ended up being pretty damn great. He didn't have the credit to take on a line of new bikes, but he did have about every oddball part out there. His shop didn't open until noon, which gave him mornings to raid rummage sales and thrift stores and bankrupt Schwinn shops around town, all the shit mechanics like me were too impatient to do. Need that upper pulley for a Huret Jubilee derailleur?

Call Musky. Pelissier Plume rear hub with French threading? He's got it. New-old-stock dust caps for it? Shit, he's got those too. But the messengers and alley cats all thought of Musky as a Dumpster mechanic. Said the guy's shop was just full of broken shit no one wanted anymore. They'd shit-talk his long, dirty beard, his grease-streaked sweatpants pulled up over his gut. Sure, there were a bunch of old creepers like Musky who owned one-man operations around town, each one more of a clusterfuck than the last. Shop-cat hair permanently stuck to all the parts, piles of bent wheels, that sort of thing. I didn't like the way the messengers treated Musky. They were always bringing in worn out Campy track parts for me to rehab and I'd just call down to Musky's shop and get all the small parts I needed for the repair. I'd drop everything into the parts washer, shine it up, reassemble it, and charge them triple just for being disrespectful to Musky.

Truck would probably try to screw him over—he didn't respect mechanics, especially elderly ones who could get even the lamest rides rolling again—just like he had me. I owed Musky. He was the only old guy I'd ever listened to. When my old man split for good my sophomore year and my family was flat broke, Musky took me on at his shop, taught me how to repair all sorts of obscure shit, made sure I didn't end up living in some crack den, smoking rock out of a broken light bulb all day like all the other kids who grew up off Burleigh. He was good with rescuing the neighborhood strays and giving them some direction. He cut me loose after I graduated high school, and told me to go work for a shop that actually made money, but I've never forgotten the late nights he spent walking me through wheel builds and overhauls.

The scrap yard guy pulled off his stocking cap and stuffed it into his pocket like he was prepping to charge.

"Hey, man," I said. "Can you just tell me if you know where this address is? I'm lost as hell."

"Fuck off, freak," he said. He picked up a spindle assembly, weighed it in his hand. "Queer. Greaser. Tattooed, queer-greaser-freak."

I folded the checkpoint flyer and stuffed it back into my pocket. "Well, now I see what your problem is. You're fucking crazy."

The guy examined the spindle assembly a moment, then side-armed the thing at me. It cracked the nub of my ankle and I toppled to the asphalt. The guy picked up another chunk of metal and started toward me. "Damn straight," he said.

Before I could find out what the second object he was going to throw at me was, I collected myself, jumped on my bike, and took off down Canal. This kind of situation is why I don't ride a fixie like all the messengers around Milwaukee: I find myself getting chased a lot—by stray pit bulls, junkyard guards, pissed-off boy-friends and husbands—so I need the extra get up and go of a full set of gears. I didn't look back to see if the old guy was gimping after me, or if he'd sent some yard-hound after me. My ankle was swelling, I could tell. I'd be wrenching on a stool for the next few weeks, but I didn't stop to assess the damage. I took the first ramp out of the Valley.

———

I hauled ass back to Bayview, back to the Bucking Bronco where Truck would be buying everyone a round to celebrate me being lost in the bowels of the city, the strong chance I'd been blasted with a shotgun. I hopped the curb, slapped the U-lock around the front wheel and the down tube, and dumped the bike in the patch of grass in front of the Bronco. The wrought iron fence out front was already crowded with posers' fixies, guys who hung around the messenger and alley cat crowd, around the back room of the shop, like they were messengers or mechanics. TJ's jalopy, a Cutlass convertible from the late '70s, custom-painted bass-boat blue, was up on the curb. The metallic flakes in the paint sparkled in the moonlight, even though the car was a total piece. The top was down, as always, because it was stuck like that. TJ was a regular at the Bronco, a local deadbeat who you never saw anywhere but there, a deadbeat who had been absorbed into Truck's inner circle. A couple of weeks before, a few of my female friends felt faint in the Bronco after being roofied, and I declared TJ the primary suspect. He didn't do shit to dispute it, even nodded a little before bringing the shell to his lips. I keyed his Cutlass before heading to the door.

Inside, I pushed through the crowd of drunks outfitted in bike garb you'd never catch me in—old-school cycling caps, wool jerseys, bargain-bin gloves. That's a nice way to get run off the road by some tea-klanner in a beater pickup. Some jerk turned around and his big-ass messenger bag clipped me and knocked me into another guy, who deposited his Pale Ale all over my shirt. When he saw I was wearing a threadbare black T-shirt, as I do every day because all wrenches know shirts just get destroyed anyway, he didn't apologize. My ankle had swollen, tightened inside my shoe, so I wasn't up for being patient with the alley cat crowd. I elbowed him in the back and forced my way to the bar where Truck was posted up.

He was having a good laugh, at my expense, with TJ and Kathryn'd. As in: "You think that's hitting rock bottom? Ever been Kathryn'd?" She was his latest girl, another one of these messenger groupies. She claimed she'd lived in all the bike-friendly cities around the world—Prague, Budapest, New York, San Francisco, Portland. And now Milwaukee. I suspected she was a bullshitter just like Truck, who made all the same claims, but was really just a fucked-up kid from a rich suburb outside Milwaukee. Truck and Kathryn'd shit-talked the *vanity* of all those other cities and claimed they liked how *real* Milwaukee was, how tight the cycling community was. They liked to hang out in all the blue-collar dive bars around the South Side, trying to prove how hardcore they were, but I saw them get thrown out more than a few times. Those old drunks, guys like my old man, may be broke and septic, but they still remember how to kick someone's ass.

"Dan-O," Truck said when he saw me. "How was the Valley? Mark this man down for a bonus point just for riding all the way out there." Everyone cheered. TJ raised his glass. Kathryn'd wrapped her tatted arms around Truck and licked the side of his face.

"Perfect. Just perfect," I said. I flicked the folded-up checkpoint flyer onto the counter and held out my hand for the next one. Truck handed me the sheet of paper, but I didn't look at it. "Just tell me where the hell you're sending me next. Where? The airport?"

"Nope. I'm done joking around now, Danny boy. This one is for real."

"The real deal," TJ added. He never had anything to say, really. Seemed like TJ was always hanging out, waiting to echo Truck. He curled one end of his Rollie Fingers-style mustache around his index finger. That stupid stache was his life's work.

I unfolded the sheet of paper and looked at the address, but it wasn't an address. It was the lighthouse on the end of the breakwater. "Seriously?"

"You'll like this one. It's a task checkpoint. There's drinking involved." Kathryn'd massaged his shoulders. "This is my finest course yet, buddy. I have all the greats working checkpoints—Bonsai, Ray, even that old crazy Musky Mueller."

I looked down, saw Musky's shop name as the sponsor of the breakwater checkpoint. Truck probably figured Musky would get into a fight with a graffiti artist out there and be hauled in for assault, or catch pneumonia and have to shutter his failing shop for good.

Of course, there weren't any bars out on the breakwater, just a dozen or so hobos pulling on tall cans of Steel Reserve sheathed in paper bags. I glanced at the marker board with the check-in times posted. There were still alley cats who hadn't returned from the first drop, guys who probably didn't really want to race in the first place.

I had a chance not to be DFL. If the breakwater turned out to be another bullshit checkpoint, I wouldn't have been all that pissed off. I knew the area, had smoked joints out on the rocks and did some bouldering. I'd grab Musky, take him out for a shell and shot, and tell him what I'd do to Truck. Plus, the last person I'd fuck with is a wrench. I speak the truth. Truck was the kind of bike-rat who owned a fleet of identical fixies for show, who spent most of his messenger paycheck on tricking them out with gold or polished parts, but didn't know an Italian-thread bottom bracket from an English. See, it wouldn't have been that hard, hand-tightening that new set of old-school Japanese track pedals he was too stupid to install himself. I wouldn't wait. I just limped outside, pulled a few emergency wrenches out of my bag, and backed off the stem bolt and axle nut on Truck's bike a quarter turn. Musky taught me it doesn't take much for a mechanic to handle people like that.

—

Now, usually I didn't like cruising up Water Street through the Third Ward after dark, not with all the drunk meatheads looking to fuck up bike geeks and artsy types, riders on electric green vintage Pinarellos like me, but it was the shortest way to the breakwater. I'd been on too many pub crawls where we got good and sauced at the VFW Post in Bayview with all the tough old birds, only to find ourselves in fistfights with dudes in dry-cleaned and pressed Oxfords. These guys had SUVs. But that wasn't the worst part about riding through the gentrified wasteland. The pigs were all younger, barflies themselves who frequented the area, so tended to jump into any brawl and clear out unwanted trash like me. These cops weren't those of my childhood, third-generation cops from West Allis and Mitchell Park and Glendale, guys who drank union beer and played lawn darts and wouldn't mind cracking gym-rat skull to help out kids from the neighborhood.

I figured it was early enough that I wouldn't run into too many drunks on the prowl for potential fistfights. The worst I'd encounter would be some chick dooring me as she fell out her Acura, maybe a last minute delivery truck unloading more kegs. I pulled my shifter to move the chain onto the big ring and stomped on the pedals of my Pinarello. A sharp pain from my ankle spiraled up my leg, but I ignored it. If I had stopped pedaling, my ankle would have swollen full and locked. I kept moving, kept it loose. The bike's bottom bracket creaked, still seized with the salt of last winter. That's the thing about being a mechanic: by the time we're done wrenching on everyone else's neglected ride, we're too damn tired to work on our own. You can hear a mechanic's bike ten blocks away, squeaking and rattling as we hit each tar bead on the road.

The light turned from yellow to red, but I blasted through the intersection anyway, just missing a bus that had jumped the light. The driver laid on the horn even though he didn't even have to brake for me. The city had been running short yellows to pick off drivers during rush hour and boost revenue, but the change really made riding through downtown a lot hairier for cyclists. I'd like to have blamed Truck for my not-so-near miss, and probably would later to the other mechanics back at the shop, but really there wasn't shit anyone could do. Short yellows. Doors. They were part of us.

I heard a car accelerate behind me. By the time I glanced over my shoulder, the corner of the bumper was nudging my heel. I tapped the front brake and steered into the gutter to give the car some space so the jackass would just cruise on past. But the driver slowed with me, scooted over to pin me between the side of the car and the curb. I bunny-hopped over a sewer grate and dodged into an alley that I regularly used as an escape route from intoxicated assholes in foreign cars when I was stupid enough to venture into the Third Ward. The networks of alleys behind the bars and restaurants were usually the way I managed to get out of the area without too much trouble. About the worst you'd find was a couple of dish-dogs hitting a pipe before returning to work. Those guys didn't like to be bothered. But I knew I was short on time, couldn't take the alleys unless I wanted to DFL, so I stopped and pulled a U-turn to return to Water.

When I wheeled around, I saw the car blocking the alley. And that the car was a beater Crown Vic, an unmarked squad car. The cop hadn't even turned on the lights, and instead abandoned the vehicle and charged at me, Taser unholstered.

"What in the hell do you think you're doing, guy?" he said. He was young, maybe early thirties, maybe late twenties but looked older, probably because his personal life was all kinds of fucked up.

"Just riding along," I said. The standard line. I braked and the shoes howled against the rim.

"Looks to me like you're doing a lot more than that," he said. He kept his hand on his Taser in case I made a break for it. "Saw you run that red back there. Then you were riding in the middle of the road."

"Sorry about the red light. But I'm pretty sure riding in the street is legal." I tried to coast past him, but he stepped in front of me and teased the Taser out of its holster a bit.

"I'd say the reckless riding and red light aren't the biggest problems here." He turned down the volume on his radio, a move that always means the cop is looking to have a little chat with you. I made a full stop and unclipped from the pedals, careful with the jacked-up ankle. I knew the routine. "You ready to tell me what you're doing?"

"No, but I'm guessing you are," I said. I wanted my ticket for whatever bullshit he was going to tag me for. I wanted the ticket so I could drop it into a Dumpster and hit my next checkpoint out on the breakwater.

He hooked his thumbs into his belt. "Clever. We know you all are having one of your bicycle races around the city. You messengers forget that's illegal. So I can either take you to jail or you can pay a $250 fine."

"Okay, so fine me," I said. I didn't flinch. The owner of the shop where I wrenched knew all the police captains downtown. The guy would get us out of anything—assault, public intox, bogus checks— but expected us to wrench for eight bucks an hour, under the table. The previous spring, he'd gotten one of the mechanics shared custody of his kids through a connection at Human Services. The bennies were solid. He was the sort of boss who'd do about anything for you: peel off a couple of twenties when you couldn't feed yourself, hook it up with a six-pack when you looked one flat repair from offing yourself in July. But he sure as hell wouldn't let you quit. Job for life and all that.

"All right then," he said. "Get off your bike and lean against my car." He escorted me over to the Crown Vic and I leaned my bike against the car. "Don't touch my car with your bicycle."

He grabbed his ticket book out of his car and came back around. "I'll need to see an ID."

I patted the pocket of my T-shirt. "Don't have one, man." Which was the truth. One of the first rules of alley cat races was that no one was allowed to keep an ID on them in case some bullshit came up. Our IDs were all rubber-banded together and safely tucked away in Truck's pocket. He made us all pick an alias in case we mouthed off to a cop too much and ended up in jail and he had to come bail us out. That was the lousiest, him having to use the purse money to bail out an alley cat with an unchecked tongue.

"I'm going to check your bag," he said. I offered him my bag and he tore through it, but came up with squat, so dropped it on my shoes. "Name," he said, pen ready.

"Grace, I said. "Chris Grace."

He twirled the pen around his fingers a moment like he was

thinking it over and looked up. "That's not your name," he said finally.

"You're right. Sorry." I searched my mind for another name, thought about all the shop tags I'd logged that week. As I thought, another alley cat cruised past and gave me the finger. "Truck," I said. "No, no, Theodore Hartmann," I said, remembering Truck's Christian name.

He scribbled down the name. A small crowd of meatheads and their brides started to circle the squad car. They liked watching people on bikes getting ticketed, especially because they knew we'd always pull some kind of stunt that would get us arrested.

"Yo, bikeman," one of the guys in the crowd said. "That guy sold me a bike last week," he said to his pals. "And now he's going to get arrested." I remembered the guy. I sold him some piece of shit mountain bike made to look like it was *extreme* and *expensive* when really anyone who knew anything about bikes knew you could never take the thing off road. I was positive the guy would try to take it on some trails and the bike would explode, so I'd get him for the cost of the bike and the repairs later. I had to call him "bro" a few times to get him to buy.

"Address," the cop said. Before I could say anything, the bike guy rifled an aluminum Bud Light bottle at the cop and it struck him right on the back of the head. The cop dropped his ticket book and turned. "You there," he said. He marched toward the crowd, Taser still unholstered, and radioed for backup.

I jumped back on the Pinarello and took off. I sprinted past the cop, knifed through the crowd, and pushed down the sidewalk. Something clicked behind me and I turned and saw the cop had discharged the Taser and the thing was pumping serious current into one of the meatheads. The cop had Truck's name and that's all he needed to know.

I hopped the curb back into the street and rocked the Pinarello back and forth to pick up speed, then cut between two cars stopped at the light. I wouldn't be stopping for any reds, not if I was going to avoid being DFL.

A siren sounded behind me. I glanced over my shoulder. Another squad car crept up to the crowd, and the cop who was going to ticket me pointed and waved him on. The driver gunned the engine and headed down the street toward me, so I ditched the street for a parking garage. I'd played enough polo during the winter to know the parking garages and alleys of downtown. Police lights flashed on the parking garage walls. The wail of sirens entered the garage. They'd probably spend the entire night cruising the streets in search of me. I'd let them hunt me. My whole life I've managed to escape. I was gone.

———

The Oakleaf Trail can be pretty damn sketchy at night if you don't have a headlight, which, of course, I'd left back at the shop. I was really trucking through the dark trail in the narrow span of trees that ran parallel to the lake because there was a good chance a cop had spotted me in Cathedral Square. A cruiser had trailed me for four blocks along Mason. The cop inside lit up the spotlight when the car pulled behind me, but I lost it when I dipped into one of the hobo-cut singletracks that led to the Oakleaf Trail. Thank the gods of urban development for the Sewer Socialists of the fifties and sixties who had the foresight to build get-away routes for people like me. Because I don't look like a messenger, the cop probably thought I was just another weirdo venturing into the woods to troll for HJs or free nuggets. They had worse shit to worry about with all those engine-nerds at MSOE drinking themselves to death in their crappy little dorm rooms.

pAnyway, I bombed down the ramp that dropped me into McKinley Park. I rocketed past the hippies slinging late night lattes at Alterra, through four lanes of traffic on Lincoln Memorial, past the shuttered charter boat huts. This checkpoint was a pretty serious haul from Bayview, so I thought there was a good chance Truck had sent me on another bullshit run. You know, I didn't mind it so much. The gale off the harbor was steady and cool, the Beamers and Porches of the Yacht Club cleared from the marina's lot. Back in high school, my friends and I would regularly ditch class and drive my rust-bucket Oldsmobile 88 down to the lake to get high, walk along the beach, and eat garbage from one of the food trucks. We never swam in Lake Michigan, of course. Half the time the city had signs posted detailing the elevated bacteria levels in the water. We'd all made the mistake of swimming in that sewage before, spent weeks bed-ridden and violently ill.

I slalomed between potholes and concrete barriers as I made my way out to the breakwater. The gate out to the breakwater's narrow walk had already been closed and chained for the night, so I hooked my bike's handlebars in the fence's fabric and locked it. Waves slapped the chunks of demoed concrete piled around the breakwater's walk. My ankle was beginning to harden to the point of uselessness. I'd jumped the breakwater's fence a couple dozen times, but never with only one good leg. I always tested my weight against the fence before going over. The thing looked like it was one fence-jumper away from folding.

Once over the fence, I squinted along the breakwater's curve to see if Musky was still sitting out in the damp cold. The silhouettes of a few graffiti artists moved along a pile of boulders. I didn't worry too much about the cops coming out to the breakwater, because everyone in the city knew every surface of the concrete had been tagged, so it was really an art gallery more than anything. Every now and then a night-fisherman would venture too far onto the rocks and slip into the water, but mostly there was no reason to patrol out there anymore. It'd been lost to graffiti.

I moved along the breakwater's concrete barriers, past boulders slicked with algae and lake-waste. A graffiti artist nodded to me as I passed and returned to tagging *Endgame*. As I rounded the corner to the last straight, I saw Musky slouched on an overturned bucket. "Musky," I called. I hobbled over to him. A beer had exploded all over the front of his Dickies insulated coverall. He looked up at me and stared for a long time before saying, "Oh. Hey there, Daniel."

He had been there for a while. Several cans of Stroh's rolled around on the ground in front of him. The wind picked up and one of the cans started end over end toward the rocks, but I caught it with my worthless foot. "Say, you look miserable. How long have you been hanging out here?"

"Fuck if I know. Long enough to polish off this here twelve-pack." He picked up a can and squinted at the label. "This is about the shittiest booze I've ever consumed. You all were supposed to drink at the checkpoint, but I believe Truck pulled one over on me." Musky pulled at his beard and zipped the leg seams down to the ankles. "He swung by the shop this afternoon to tell me about the alley cat. Said he'd set me up with a checkpoint and that it'd be good advertising for my shop."

I crushed the cans and made a little pile of them so they wouldn't blow into the lake. The lake had enough cans and plastic bags wildlife would get caught up in. "Yeah, he fucked me over too. Sent me down to the Valley. I wrecked my ankle riding through there."

"I've always said there's nothing but hoarders and junk dealers down there. No one listens to me." He picked up a can, pressed it to his lips, and turned it over to see if anything was left. "Well, that Truck is a little shit. His old man used to race time trials, you know. Never had a car worth more than a couple hundred bucks. He used to just sell his cars for scrap because he couldn't find anyone foolish enough to buy one. There was a whole row of his junkers down in the Valley."

A kid with a hoodie draped over his body walked past us. He

stopped a few feet behind Musky, leaned down, and sprayed his tag. Musky turned around on the bucket and said to the kid, "That's illegal you know. All these goddamn tags. You really think anyone is going to remember you?"

The kid mumbled something and Musky stood, but I horse-collared him before he could get anywhere near the kid. Last thing I needed was Musky going after a pissed-off teenager with a utility knife. The kid held up his can of spray paint and blasted it in Musky's direction, but the wind caught the paint and sent a blue mist across the front of his sweatshirt. "Motherfuckers," he said. The kid must have felt sorry for what he'd done, or maybe he thought we looked mean enough to do some real damage to him. He scrambled over the rocks and disappeared.

Musky pushed me off him. "I'd have struck him," he said. "Struck him down." He slipped a utility knife out of his pocket and waved it at me. "Would have taught that child a lesson about respect. That's the problem, you see. These kids don't respect elders none."

"Easy, Musky," I said. I took the utility knife from him and tossed it into the boulders. The thing was plastic and flimsy anyway, a cheap-shit tool that told me his shop was hemorrhaging. If there's one thing a bike mechanic doesn't chintz out on, it's a utility knife. I've seen far too many newbies fuck around with a plastic knife only to have the blade slip and jam into their hand or slice their thumb down to the bone. I have a knot of scar tissue on my thumb to show how I learned this.

"That gate down there still open? I'd like to get the hell off of here and get a George Webb burger into me."

"I'll help you over the fence," I said. I picked up the can of spray paint and considered tagging my name alongside the others, but restrained myself because I didn't want any memory of my alley cat career. We headed down the walk to shore, Musky clipping right along, me dragging my ruined ankle behind me.

Headlights cut across the parking lot. The engine rattled as the driver accelerated toward the gate. Only one car engine in the city shook that much, and that car belonged to TJ. They were rolling five, six deep from what I could tell.

Musky held up a moment, looked up at the group unloading from the car, and kept moving toward the fence. "Buddies are here," he said without turning back to me.

I knew why they were there. I could see Truck's face, the gash above his eyebrow from where he had wrecked after his front wheel disconnected from the bike. He'd probably stopped up the bleeding with a dirty bar rag, held it up there as he walked toward the fence.

"Dan-O, Dan-O, Dan-O," Truck said. He pulled the bar rag away from his face, pitched it in the direction of a municipal trash barrel. Sure enough, the gash had parted his right eyebrow. Truck never wore a helmet.

"We have some things to settle, Dan-O," Truck said.

Behind him I could see TJ fish out a loose two-by-four from his back seat. He twirled the board around like a baton, slung it over his shoulder, and moved to join the rest of his group. Musky stopped again and patted his pockets in search of the utility knife, but quit, probably remembering. Somewhere behind us, the knife was down deep in the crevices between the rocks, forever lost. I stood next to Musky and watched Truck's gang start to climb the fence. I inventoried my bag in my head: set of Allen wrenches, fifteen millimeter open-end, a dying Sharpie. I turned, calculated the distance to the end of the breakwater, to the lighthouse throwing its beacon out into Lake Michigan. Truck and his crew crested the fence. They would come at us full on. I shook the can of spray paint and the pea clanked around inside. I readied my finger on the trigger and set myself between Musky and Truck, right where I belonged.

Scrap

The waiver Flint signed failed to mention the voids in his vision would be permanent. He had snagged the gig testing video games through some temp agency out in Culver City. Even though he'd never played more than a few minutes of a video game in his life, he was hired to sit in a cubicle and play virtual hole after virtual hole of a golf game in development. The temp agency said it was a good way for the ligament damage in his knee to heal after a decorative rock bounced off of a dump truck at a job site and mangled his leg. The game company supplied the temps with leather office chairs, unlimited fountain drinks, and all the day-old bagel they could stuff themselves with. In the two months he slaved away over the game console, his knee's swelling eased little and he gained ten, fifteen pounds, easy.

When Flint crossed the street to his building, he found his father—good old Coach Raymond—sitting on the front stoop, his second unannounced visit this spring. Summer was fast approaching, the morning marine layer over the Pacific burning off earlier each day, and he knew why Raymond had rolled into town from Milwaukee. Teams around the League would start sorting through the discards and signing guys off the street for training camp, guys who'd been laying asphalt or throwing stock or degreasing rotisseries at a chicken shack. Camp bodies, that's what they were called. Guys who put in four decent years at some tier-two college program, maybe had already been to a camp or two, played some arena ball, and were signed for the real pros to beat up on. They'd suffer through late hits, punches in the gut, cleats to the hand, only to be released with shredded ligaments and an injury settlement that wouldn't cover all the final notices they had ignored while at camp. Camp bodies. Guys like Flint.

Raymond spent his winter as he had since Flint left a year early from Fresno State: sending him League-approved nutritional supplements and Flint's old game tapes from college and the ten plays from the lone preseason game he played for the Raiders three years ago. Flint didn't even own a TV, let alone a VCR. He had told him to stop burning his retirement fund on Priority postage, but his old man just kept the tapes coming. One, sometimes two, a week.

Raymond looked up from the *LA Weekly* he must have swiped out of the newsstand chain-locked to the lamppost. He rolled up the paper and stuck it into the scrubby hedge. "Goddamn. As I thought. You've grown doughy and irrelevant." Raymond pinched his belly. "Just look at you."

Flint swatted away Raymond's arm. "You're looking pretty shitty yourself." And he did. Despite the green faded to teal, he still wore that ridiculous Wauwatosa East windbreaker with "Coach Channing" stitched underneath the offensive cartoon Native American logo the school retired fifteen years ago. Raymond still brought in a little dough by coaching receivers, but had been forced into early retirement by the Public Works department after spending thirty-five years trouncing through the sludge of the aging sewers beneath the city. He ate the same lunch—two beef dogs from the cart on Kilbourn—every day and ignored his Type II diabetes.

"When do you head back?" Flint asked.

"I'm not answering that. Had some time before camp and I thought I'd come out here to see what kind of shape you were getting yourself in. Apparently none."

"I jacked up my knee again hauling stone a while back," Flint said.

Raymond glanced down at the compression sleeve around his knee.

"What did I tell you about hard labor?"

"Keeps me fit," Flint lied. What Raymond didn't realize was he didn't have many options beyond trolling Craigslist jobs. He hadn't gone to trade school and hadn't finished his degree at Fresno because Raymond coaxed him into training for camp tryouts rather than going to class. Raymond said he was primed for the League and wouldn't ever need the degree. And when he went back to school, he saw how many upper division credits short he was, that his scholarship had dried up. Then he saw what normal people shelled out for out-of-state tuition and decided that was enough. He moved to Venice Beach and had been working lousy jobs, mostly unskilled labor through the temp agency. Recently, he collected scrap for cash under the table.

Raymond hiked his shorts, adjusted his windbreaker, and pulled his ball cap off his head. You could barely see Flint's name and old jersey number through all the salt rings on the hat. "I got in touch with Houston Crow. He phoned the coach with that arena team up in LaCrosse. They could use someone with good hands. Houston says he may be able to get you back into the League with some new tape."

"I'm enjoying my retirement."

"Retirement? Some retirement you got here. Crappy studio with a toilet that don't flush right. Doing your dishes in the same sink you brush your teeth in. No career. You had a good thing going and you fucked it up. Quit feeling sorry for yourself."

"Shit, Dad. I haven't played a down in three years," Flint said. He hoped Raymond wouldn't bring up his stint with the Muncie Mastodons, a team that signed him, bum knee and all, after the Raiders cut him loose. The team was always teetering on the brink of destruction—the owner always pulled for them to lose so he had to cut checks for only fifty bucks instead of the two-fifty they received if they won. But the team sucked—twenty farm kids with crustaches who couldn't even plant and go—so the guy never had to worry about paying out. Maybe five of the players played college ball and actually knew what the hell they were doing. Locals would show up to drink discounted skunk-brews leftover from the County Fair, watch the visiting team crack amateur skull.

Flint suited up for five games with the failing franchise, if that's even what you could call it. He found work at a grain distributor two days a week, which didn't even cover rent, and trotted out every Friday to play both ways for the Mastodons. Until he shredded his knee, again, after he caught a tear in the arena's ancient Astroturf.

One of the local surfers walked past, gave Flint a little arm tap, and said, "Hey." Flint had bought her two-dollar mimosas a few mornings after she'd raged it through the night and stumbled into the breakfast place off the Walk.

"Oh, I see now. You're out here just chasing these silicone sisters." He shook his head and pulled out a cigarette, but Flint plucked it out of his hand before he could light it.

"The super doesn't want cigarettes around the building. You left a whole mess of butts along the walk last time you visited."

"You've grown soft. That's what Houston figured would happen to you. He's a sharp agent."

"Yeah. He's done so much for me." Flint never cared for Houston Crow, the pot-bellied sports agent Raymond dug up through some mutual friend. Houston's headliner clients were a pair of washed-up gunslinger quarterbacks who spent most of their careers lobbing balls over in NFL Europa, and three or four thirty-something infielders who couldn't break through the double-A ceiling. Houston had a dingy little office down in Cincinnati that Flint visited after Raymond persuaded him to try for the League. They took Houston's junker Beemer to the nearest Skyline Chili, where Flint had to witness Houston shovel forkfuls of the chili that wasn't really chili into his mouth, occasionally dropping dollops of the sludge onto the agent contract Flint was going to have to sign. Houston, along with Raymond's endorsement, was responsible for stranding Flint in Muncie for that winter. And he always took his fifteen percent cut from the fifty-dollar game check.

"Well, I could use some rest," Raymond said. "I sat next to the most miserable little shit you've ever met on the plane. Kid kept pulling at my ear."

"Sure thing, Dad." Flint unlocked the security door to his building and Raymond started up the stairs, stopping every ten or so steps to catch his breath. Flint watched, blinked several times until the voids cleared and his focus returned, and waited until his father disappeared up the staircase.

———

Admiral Lou honked his truck's horn and flashed the headlights in the street below, signaling Flint had scrap work that night. He opened the window, stuck out his hand, and flipped Lou the bird to acknowledge he'd be down in a minute. Raymond was flopped out face down on Flint's mattress on the floor, his stomach still growling as it digested the street burritos Flint had fetched for dinner earlier. He'd be out with Lou for five, six hours and return before Raymond woke from his food coma.

He'd been working nights for Lou off and on for a year now, riding along in Lou's retired Penske truck, rough brushstrokes of black over the old Penske logo. They stayed mostly quiet as they drove around L.A. to collect scrap in the night. They made a solid two-man crew, Lou lugging the smaller pieces of scrap to the truck, Flint working the Bosch grinder to break down the more serious pieces—rebar beam cages, blown commercial water heaters, pierced propane tanks. He didn't know exactly how the hell Lou found out about scrap, but they'd cruise around the industrial streets of L.A., past metal fabricators and machine shops, and there the scrap would be, dumped outside the security fence.

Lou was one tough motherfucker with a steady stream of tales to go with his attitude. He claimed he captained a few hundred container ships from China to the Port of Los Angeles, fought off neo-pirates in the Indian Ocean, caught a group of armed freeloaders from Cambodia crowded into a shipping cargo. He kept a revolver underneath the driver's seat, but Flint always figured Lou felt a little more at ease working with a partner. They would run into the occasional scrap-poacher out there in the darkness, men desperate and willing enough to have a fistfight with someone over a busted washing machine. The third time Flint went out to collect scrap, they were jumped by a group of teenagers out looking for discarded pipe and sheet metal. Lou scooped up a section of stray copper tubing and struck one of the kids right across the back of his bare skull. The jagged end of the tubing tore a hole in the kid's flesh, left a wound that looked like a star. The other kids bailed down the alleys and narrow streets. That industrial park had been clear of poachers since.

He took his hinged knee brace out of the front closet and went downstairs to meet Lou. The cool air from the Pacific had rolled in. If he was going to do hard labor, it was best done at night, when the heat of the day lifted and his vision was better. The dim moonlight eased the stress on his blown-out eye, and the constellations of voids faded to the point of no longer being noticeable. Despite his many formal written requests and in-person follow-ups with the coordinator at the temp agency, he couldn't seem to bully his way onto a road crew that worked nights under a halogen sun, so scrap work would have to do.

Lou unrolled the window. "Who's the fatso in the window?" he asked, tilting his head up to Flint's apartment.

Flint turned and saw Raymond standing in the faint light of the apartment, staring at the truck in the street below. Raymond had shed the windbreaker and now had only a threadbare tank-top stretched over his wide belly. He pulled at his ear lobe, then turned from the window and retreated out of view.

"My old man's up there," Flint said. He opened the passenger's side door and hoisted himself up into the truck's cab, which stank of the bowl Lou had just cashed. Lou wasn't much for sharing.

"Looks like a man without much fight left in him."

"He received some terrible news today."

Lou nodded, jammed the key into the ignition, and started the truck. He threw the truck into drive and gunned it down the block. Flint noticed Lou's hand was wrapped in a wad of bloodied paper towel, which he'd secured with a few layers of duct tape. "What the hell happened to your hand?"

Lou held up the club-hand. "This. This is my useless hand." He thumped the mangled hand against the steering wheel, then winced. "I got cheap last night and flew solo. The Bosch slipped and tore right into the side of my hand, down to the bone. Thought I lost a pair of fingers, but just ended up with a big flap of skin. I have five butterfly bandages underneath this mess."

"Should have gotten that stitched up," Flint said, though he knew Lou probably didn't have health insurance and didn't want to see half his scrap money go to some medical billing facility in the Central Valley each month.

"Eh, doctors," Lou said. "Anyway, that's the last time I do a job without you. I think you'll dig what's up tonight: Cal Mast Company."

Cal Mast usually meant a big haul and a handsome payout. They manufactured aluminum spars right there in-house, and managed to screw up every few. They'd drag the rejected spars and masts outside the gates and lean them against the fence for Lou and Flint to drag away during the night. With his cut of the action, Flint would be able to buy Raymond brunch along the beach tomorrow, a Bloody Mary and three-egg omelet, and convince him to fly home early. He'd try to tell Raymond there wasn't much use in him staying, in spending money on postage for the tapes and plane tickets anymore.

"Hector at Cal Mast is a big Raiders fan, you know," Lou said. "Still talks about that one time he got to meet you. He's always asking if you're looking to play again."

"Don't really remember the guy, to be honest," Flint said, slipping the knee brace onto his leg. But he did remember the man, remembered how he slapped him hard on the bicep and peppered him with questions about recent Raiders draft busts, Al Davis, and, my god, when the hell is Al going to come to his senses and bring the team back to LA? Hector droned on for several minutes before he stabbed his index finger into Flint's sternum, looked around the work yard to make sure none of his employees were looking on, and said, "I have something I want to show you." Hector then slipped off his Dickies shop shirt and turned to show Lou and Flint his back. Through the thicket of dark back hair, Hector had "Commitment to Excellence" inked across his shoulders. "That's my business philosophy," Hector said as he struggled to push his left arm through a shirtsleeve. Once Hector finally had the shirt on and adjusted he said, "I'll tell you this much. If I ever made to camp with the Raiders, I'd make damn sure Al never cut me."

As if Flint had a say in the matter. He spent his final semester at Fresno skipping the classes he needed to graduate in order to train. He ran route trees at a local high school with a League veteran who the Broncos had pink-slipped the previous season. He played slot receiver in the Texas vs. The Nation game, hauled in three passes over the middle, but still went undrafted. When the call came from some low-level personnel assistant with the Raiders, he had just returned to Milwaukee, thinking he would follow in the family trade inspecting cracked sewer pipes below the city. At the airport, Raymond punched him in the back and said, "Just win, baby!" which seemed about the most predictable thing he could have said to a son who was going to camp with the Raiders. Seven hours later, there he was in Oakland being fit with the Silver and Black. He caught a glimpse of Mr. Davis himself—eyes shielded by dark sunglasses, the light glinting off the diamonds on his watch—as an assistant showed him the facility.

Flint pulled at the Velcro straps on his knee brace and secured it. He worried the knee would crumble any day now, the structural elements shredded, and he would be left to scrounge for some bullshit clerical job at an office out in the Valley staffed by men and women in unisex polo shirts and Dockers khakis.

"Hope you're ready to haul some serious scrap," Lou said. "Maybe I should have found someone a little more stout to ride along for this one."

Even though Flint measured just 5'9 and a buck eighty, he could run a mean slant, and Mr. Davis recognized that. Mr. Davis had always built his teams around the League's discards—veterans who'd be kicked off other teams for carrying guns without permits, talking shit about owners to the media, and the college nameless leftover after the draft's dust had settled. And so Flint practiced hard. He refused assistance from the medical staff and instead taped his wrists and ankles himself in the auxiliary locker room for roster long shots. When he would catch a linebacker moving laterally toward a running back, he'd lower his shoulder and level him. He stiff-armed nickelbacks in the facemask, clipped safeties at the knees downfield. Mr. Davis sent an assistant over, a young kid in a foam visor, to tell Flint that Mr. Davis liked the way he played the game.

What did him in was a kick return in the fourth quarter of a meaningless preseason game. The punt sailed high, hung in the air for a moment before rocketing down to him. He fielded it, juked the first gunner, and darted through a gap in the coverage. He had three, maybe four coverage guys to beat when he reached the Coliseum's infamous infield dirt leftover from the A's. When he went to cut, he felt something in his knee let go, not so much a pop as a shift, realignment for the worse.

Team doctors told him the repair would be routine, rehab six to eight months, and then he'd be right back on the field. Somewhere else.

Lou ran a red light and took a sharp right onto the 10 without slowing. Flint caught an advertisement for Manny Ramirez's home run total on a billboard, but the actual total fell into one of the voids in his vision. He'd heard somewhere that the Dodgers were thinking about cutting Manny loose after the season, saying he'd lost a little bat speed, his contract a drain on the team's ability to sign younger talent.

"Say, Lou," Flint said. "I thought I'd let you know I'm going looking for other work. Just in case you need to find a backup for me or something."

Lou ignored him and shifted across two lanes of traffic without signaling.

"Oh, before I forget," Lou said after a while. He pulled a pair of ratty twenties out of his pocket and flicked them onto Flint's lap. "Here's a little extra from that haul last week. Consider it a roster bonus."

—

Raymond waited two days to tell him his second cousin Chuck was missing, not that Flint gave a shit. Uncle Butch requested that Raymond check in on Chuck, who lived clear out in the Valley with the porno-starlets and Oil Tycoons and slick Mercedes salesmen. Flint still thought of Chuck as the feral little white trash kid of their youth—always barefoot, shirtless, rattail bouncing as he ran away from adult supervision. Chuck followed him out to California, followed him up to Napa for training camp with the Raiders, then along the 1 all the way to Venice Beach, where Flint retreated to have his knee put back together. Flint didn't even have any furniture for his efficiency when Chuck pounded on the door and asked, without really asking, could he stay until he got back on his feet.

There Chuck was boozing it on the floor in the corner while Flint sat on the couch with his repaired knee elevated, waiting for the swelling to go down so he could walk around the canals, maybe even get away from Chuck and enjoy a couple of Coronas along the beach one afternoon. In trade for rent, Flint demanded that Chuck prepare meals and run errands. But every time Flint would give Chuck a couple of bucks, he would come back with a six-pack of High Life and a box of frozen Taquitos. So when Flint was finally mobile, he had to evict Chuck by force; he horse-collared him one morning without notice, and deposited him in the gutter of beach-trash outside the building.

He knew Raymond didn't really care much about Chuck and his cobbled-together life in California, but asked to look in on Chuck to fill the time in his visit. And so Flint begged his neighbor across the hall to let him borrow his Volkswagen Rabbit that had been modified for time trial racing long ago and wasn't entirely street legal. He offered the twenties Lou had given him as a deposit. They were stuck in traffic on the 405 by ten.

"Honestly, I don't know what you all are doing out here," Raymond said, raising his head over the car in front of them as if he could see how long the line of traffic extended, as if the point at which the congestion thinned could be known.

"Weather, for one," Flint said. He steered the car into the shoulder to go around a disabled Neon, then ended up riding the shoulder to the Skirball exit. The Rabbit didn't have much life left in it, and he hoped it wouldn't quit on the climb up to Mulholland and down to Ventura.

"Well, at the very least I could get you onto the staff at 'Tosa East. We need someone to coach linebackers."

"You know I don't like children, Dad."

"I was just suggesting it. Suggesting you do something with your life other than chasing fame or whatever the hell you've been doing out here. By the looks of it, you haven't been taking care of that knee."

Flint was fucking around with the Velcro on his knee brace.

"When I think of what you could be—returning kicks on Sunday afternoons for the Raiders, hauling in passes for the Vikings. Any team. Any team would have you if you just showed a little life."

Flint pressed on the gas pedal and the car jolted, rattled, and didn't pick up. He took it easy up to Mulholland, took a left and settled in behind a grandmotherly woman in a Camry. Celebrities were always throwing their cars off this road and for a moment he thought about doing the same. If his body were forever damaged, damaged to the point of complete uselessness, then Raymond would back off. Then again, Raymond would probably have to be his caretaker, force him to coach, set him up on a wheelchair along the 'Tosa East sideline.

"One of those smart pro coaches may have moved you to defense. I always thought you'd make a hell of a corner."

Flint took the curves of Mulholland at a leisurely pace, let Raymond take in the view of the Valley in whole. Somewhere down there thousands of personal assistants like Chuck were driving their junky cars around the tangled streets, balancing coffee and dry cleaning and twenty-dollar takeout lunches. Flint could never bring himself to do something that low, hustling for someone else for the free rent.

"Where the hell is this place?" Raymond said. "We're on the edge of a goddamn cliff and I don't see no fancy houses nearby."

The tree-cover broke. Without slowing, he turned the car down a residential street and eased off the brakes. They barreled down to the Valley. Raymond gripped the door handle and center console, extended his legs, wedged his feet just underneath the glove compartment, and braced for an impact. Flint let go of the steering wheel for a moment just to see if Raymond would reach for it.

He did. "Goddamn. This city's made you crazy. I'm taking a cab home. No chance in hell you'll see me back in a vehicle with you behind the wheel."

The street began to level out and Flint slowed to find the house where Chuck worked. By all reports, Chuck had a pretty good set-up with his new gig: He was the house boy for a couple who were regulars on some teen drama filmed up in Vancouver, so they weren't around much. They gave Chuck free reign over their guesthouse in the backyard and asked that he made sure to let the pool guy and landscapers in every Wednesday, drop the occasional splash of chlorine into the pool if the pH level started to stray before the pool guy was scheduled to show. The job was ideal for an idler like Chuck, who had faked a serious heroin addiction after Flint booted him out so he could crash in a treatment center rent-free for a few weeks.

Flint pulled into the house's driveway and tapped the security gate with the Rabbit's bumper.

"So how do we get into this place?" Raymond asked. "These people must be pretty damn loaded if they have a wall around their place."

"Everyone has a wall around their place here, Dad."

Raymond looked around, nodded, and stepped out of the car. "Thought the house would be a lot nicer," Raymond said. "Especially for a couple of celebrities." The house was a '50s-era ranch like the rest of the neighborhood, save for the few lots where investors had bulldozed the ranch and slapped together a mock-Med mansion. The Valley was changing, losing the character homes that made it such a desirable place to live, which was one of the many reasons why Flint tended to avoid the area.

Flint stepped onto a concrete flowerpot, then tested his weight on the gate's call box. He grabbed the top of the wall and pulled himself over without much effort. Some wall. He was half-expecting to be greeted by a neglected purebred something or other, but the yard was relatively quiet. Raymond rattled the gate, so he punched the button to release the lock.

"I wouldn't be surprised if the cops show up," Raymond said. "This is breaking and entering, you know."

"You're the one who wanted to check in on Chuck." Flint led Raymond along the side of the house to the backyard where he figured he'd find Chuck, morning martini in hand, lounging on posh outdoor furniture. But the yard was quiet. An inflatable alligator floated in the pool. Flint went over to the main house's French doors and looked inside. He placed his palms on both sides of his face to cut the glare off the glass. The voids in his vision narrowed and the house's interior came into focus. The place looked like it was set up for a magazine shoot, fake pears in a bowl on the coffee table, antique books opened to the exact middle pages to appear as though casually read. The couple was in all the professional black and white photographs on the walls, many of which featured them nude and rolling around on a beach. In one beach series, they took turns pinning each other.

When Flint turned to find Raymond, he was entering what

looked like a converted garage in the backyard. He called to Raymond, but he didn't respond. Over the pool's waterfall, he heard him say, "Goddamn," and so headed toward the building. He stopped in the doorway and took in the garage that the couple had converted into a professional-quality home theater, complete with movie theater seats and a popcorn machine. "Now this is luxury," Raymond said, scooping some stale popcorn into his hand. "I thought that cousin of yours always was a little on the slow side, but he may be onto something here, Flint."

"I don't think you should be eating these people's popcorn," Flint said. He refused to cross the door's threshold in case a home security team with mace and Tasers suddenly showed up to investigate the opened door.

"You know," Raymond said, chewing. "Had you decided to try again for the League, you could have had something like this. This could be yours." He held out his arms, spun around once, and tossed a piece of popcorn into his mouth. "May not be too late for you, kid."

Raymond picked up the remote and took a seat in the front row. He waved the remote around and clicked until the projector came on. The sudden burst of light tripped the voids in Flint's vision. He turned away, walked down the flagstone path over to the guesthouse, and looked inside. The place was empty. Despite his cousin's unreliable, freeloading nature, he envied the guy. Chuck possessed the ability to slip from one life to another in order to avoid pursuit. Eventually this sort of behavior made his immediate family back home stop chasing him and gave him the ability to choose to go after what mattered to him, even if he wasn't sure what that was yet.

He walked back over to the theater's doorway and found Raymond still reclined in one of the chairs. Several men were engaged in a firefight on the screen. After Raymond left, he decided he'd gather all the game tapes Raymond had sent, watch them, then package them in a large box and ship them back. He'd go down to the post office, sign up for a P.O. box, and tell Raymond the tapes would be safer sent there. He would never go back to that post office.

Raymond's shape was illuminated by the firelight on the screen. Flint's vision filled with voids until he could barely make out his surroundings. He held his gaze toward Raymond though, held it long enough for the shape of his father to dim.

Critters

 I stayed up late and listened for the scrape of the first plow blade against my street. The forecaster on the television said the storm was the real deal. Radar showed a heavy brushstroke of blue right over Milwaukee. Outside, snow had been falling heavy and steady, but the wind started to pick up and blow around the accumulation. The best kind of storm for plow drivers like me. I knew the snow manager would dispatch us, the second wave drivers, in an hour or so and I would waste the early morning driving the snowplow around the same neighborhood, racking up overtime.

A Honda Civic drifted down the street and pulled over in front of my building. My girlfriend Elise was sitting on the passenger side, as she had been every night for the last two weeks. I dropped another splash of Jim Beam into my travel mug of Folgers. These dudes from the restaurant—deadbeats, mostly—had been giving her rides home after their shift. The Civic was the official automobile of dish dogs in the city, guys on prison release who would blast the bits of foie gras and pools of jus from the plates bused back from the dining room. In the summer, they would squander their entire paychecks on racing slicks and try to win the money back in time trials around Miller Park.

And they were all chasing the pastry chef in residence, the girl from Paris, my Elise. After they all got off their shift, they would pile into their pack of Civics and tear ass over to one of the taverns that closed at three. They would get her shitfaced on rail whiskey and PBRs and teach her how to shoot stick, gentlemen that they were. They would take turns drunk-driving her home and hope a storm was due to hit and my boss had called me in to plow the streets.

The driver leaned over to Elise's seat. I couldn't tell if they were hugging or licking face or what. A small tornado of snow twisted through the cones of light from the gas station across the street. It lifted the tarp off the Christmas trees stacked in the gas station's parking lot.

Elise and I had been shacking up for six months. I have to admit I had a tough time creating space for another person in my dumpy one-bedroom. One of my chef friends had introduced us. He was trying to get with her, but Elise wasn't interested in a man who'd had fifteen kitchen jobs in five years. She was fresh off a plane from Paris, on loan for a year from some famous French pastry chef's kitchen, which gave our relationship an expiration date. One of the Gucci restaurants downtown had contracted her to teach them how to make baguette and desserts like the Frenchies. Even though she made her living as a pastry chef, she was small and thin. She claimed she had done a little modeling when she was younger, before she grew "fat," but I assumed that was a line every French woman could pull off with American men. She didn't belong in Milwaukee. She spent her first week living in a flat on the Eastside crowded with line cooks and junior sous chefs, guys I knew from the warehouse jobs I'd had in my twenties. They had all gotten clever and tatted themselves up with obscure band logos and took jobs in shitty kitchens. They thought they could cook their way out of the garage apartments of their youth. But I toughed it out, stayed in Bayview, and finally landed a gig with DPW Sanitation Services. I had a union card and bennies and a steady paycheck. I could afford to buy girls drinks, and I bought Elise many that first night. She stayed with me every night for a few weeks and slowly migrated her belongings into my apartment the way any girl does when she's moving in with you but pretending she's not.

I didn't want to talk to her when she finally decided to come inside, so I decided to head into the garage early and throw darts in the break room until the snow manager sent me out. She was still sitting in the Civic. Hell, she could have spent all night in there. I pulled on my boots and slipped on my coat. I went into the kitchen and took the bottles of New Glarus out of the fridge and hid them underneath the trash bag in the wastebasket. Elise had been getting so drunk she would wake up every morning and hurl into the trash-can beside the mattress in the bedroom first thing.

I killed the rest of my coffee and grabbed the bag of ice melt by the door. I started out the door but my heel crushed one of the bulbs on the loose strand of Christmas lights Elise had set near the door as a reminder for me to put them up. I wasn't one for decorations, but she thought the Milwaukee kitsch was a "nice thing." I kicked the broken glass and strand to the side and went outside. Our walk was already iced-over. I tossed a few handfuls of ice melt onto the concrete and followed the trail to my car. Elise grew up in the south of France among the sunflowers and Bordeaux vines so she didn't have ice-legs. She needed a clear walk to get home.

Elise must have seen me shuffling down the walk, because she got out of the car. She held out her arms. "This is crappy stuff," she said.

"The snow?" I said. "Get used to it." It was late December and we hadn't even gotten blasted yet. She had no idea what was coming to her.

"You have not made the lights on the house," she said.

"Put them on the house, you mean. The landlady won't allow it," I said.

I threw down a solid base of ice melt so she could manage the walk when she had to go to her shift the next morning. She skated to me and stood right up close to my face. The dishwasher was still hanging out, his Civic piping exhaust into the cold air.

"I do not feel nice," she said. She leaned in and sniffed me. "You smell like a drink."

"And you smell like the Pelt. I'm going to work," I said. I turned away and walked to my truck. She stank of Schlitz and menthols so I knew she had been at Bernie's Pelt, a shitty tavern in Pigsville that continued to serve after closing time. You know you pissed away a decade of your life with alcohol when you can smell someone and tell what bar in town they've been to that night.

I unlocked my truck's door. Elise struggled to get up the walk. The guy in the Civic sat there, probably making up a blunt to smoke with Elise after I left. Elise stopped at the little steps on the walk and turned to me. I wasn't going to leave until the guy was gone.

"This is a shitty place," she said to me across the yard. "Your city is a shitty place."

———

By the time I strolled into the Canal Street garage at DPW, the sky was absolutely shitting snow. The snow manager had called in contract welders to make spot repairs on busted plow blades. I changed into my overalls and went out onto the garage floor. Chunky Chris was in front of my roll-over blade, welding a busted plate seam. He had grown up in the worst neighborhood imaginable, the kind of neighborhood where the fire department opened up fire hydrants during the heat waves and teenagers slashed tires for sport. Now the guy made almost six figures welding stainless steel dairy drums. He was doing spot work for the city to save up for a fat rock for his girlfriend's chubby ring finger. He could knock out a whole shift's worth of work in a couple hours. He said he wanted to buy his girl the biggest goddamn ring anyone in Milwaukee had ever seen, the kind of ring Elise would get when she headed back to France, settled down, and found a Parisian with some dough in the vault.

I stared at the torch's arc for a moment and turned away. I had constellations of light in my vision.

My boss Alger came out of the office when he saw me. "The first gritter has arrived," he said. "Get in your truck, sweetheart. Bayview is a disaster. The phones are blowing up."

Gritters. That's what Alger called his favorite drivers. He was raised in the UK—in Manchester or Stoke-on-Trent or some grit-shit city—and flashed British street-speak when he was worked up about something. He respected us, the gritters. He assigned the new Mack CL rigs with heated seats to us and sent us out into the storm for twelve hours straight and didn't make us come back into the garage for union-mandated fifteens. The thing about us gritters was Alger didn't have to babysit us. We were raised in these neighbor-hoods and knew every city-owned lot, back alley, and speed bump. We made car islands and the residents didn't give a shit because they knew they had fucked up by not moving their car for snow removal. They would wave to us, call off work, and head to the tavern. We stayed in the driver's seat and pounded coffee and cleared the snow from the city streets before the morning commute.

Chris was finishing up with the plow. Across the garage, mechan-ics had started to fit plows on to garbage trucks, a sign the snow manager expected the storm to bury to city. I checked all the hydraulics on the Mack for leaks because the union boss was getting on us about our pre-ride checklist.

Alger walked over and pushed me toward the door of the cab. "Stop your bullshitting with the truck and get out there already, Moose," he said.

"I'll get there when I get there," I said. "The clown from the union office has written me up twice for not initialing the forms before driving."

"It's not your job to worry about that," he said. He studied me from a moment and clicked his pen. "You look beat. You knock up your old lady?"

"Quit it, man."

"That French woman has torn the goddamn soul out of you," he said.

He was right. In the first few months I had been with Elise, I had shed thirty pounds because of a straight liquor diet. Elise didn't understand the diet of my people. When I would bring a cheeseburger home after work, she would call me fat and throw it into the front lawn. She would cuss me out in what I imagined was Parisian slang.

"Well, she'll be back in France soon enough. I suggest you get your shit together," Alger said. "I'm assigning you a ride along."

"Fuck no you're not," I said. We had only one ride along, a tired old gimp named Donny Beller who had managed to get hired after thirty years of rejected applications to DPW. Word was HR finally taken him on because no one else would agree to start as a sorter in e-waste. But Donny didn't give a shit. He'd spent a year breaking down blown Zeniths and Gateway monitors to ship to remote villages in China so they could strip the components for precious metals. He had a wheeze from breathing in all that lead and cadmium and shit no one could pronounce. But, hell, it got him on as a trainee for snow crew, the job he'd wanted all along.

"Hey, Donny," Alger called. Donny was staring at a first aid kit on the wall. He was chewing on a Styrofoam cup of coffee. "Donny," Alger said again. He waved Donny over. "Fucking useless."

"Dammit, Alger," I said. "Guy is on the clock and just staring at shit."

"Deal with it. Teach him a little something out there. Besides, I hear he's good company."

———

Donny was a slob, the exact type of man I didn't want to share my cab with. He was known around the garage for being a bit vulgar. Not in the way everyone else around the garage was, just more awkward. At first, everyone thought he had Tourette's.

"I like a thick bitch myself," Donny said out of nowhere. He had been shelling pistachios all over my clean cab. He stopped and demonstrated the width of his preferred hindquarters with his hands in case I was curious. "Lots of them types in this neighborhood."

"You always talk like this?" I said.

"Like what, bucko?"

"Nevermind." I pulled the lever and dropped the blade. The salt spreader was dumping salt at a pretty good rate, so I trimmed it back a bit. I didn't want to drive back in to the garage to reload.

"Here, you need some pistachios," Donny said. He dumped a pile into my lap.

"Fucking hell, Donny," I said. I brushed the pistachios onto the floor. "You're not supposed to shell and drive, dude."

"Righty. Righty, Righty."

I didn't understand why the hell this guy was in my cab, why the hell the city counted this as paid training. He wasn't doing a damn thing. The guy was forty-five, had worked for every abrasive distributor and small machine manufacturer in the city. He still wore the white Oxford he'd bought for his first interview, apparently, a tight thing that compressed the fat around his neck and had yellowed armpits. He finished the shirt off with an '80s-style knit tie that had a big barbeque sauce stain and a flat end. For some reason, he showed up to work with an old-school hand-grip briefcase.

Some guys in the garage claimed they picked the lock one day. Rumor was he kept a bag of pistachios, the latest *Playboy,* a fresh undershirt, and a miniature backgammon set in there.

My phone buzzed: a text from Elise. She had been drunk-texting me every time there was a storm and I had to pull a long shift. *You have broken the lights. This is a sad thing.*

"Message from home, bucko?" Donny said, nodding. "Yeah. You know. I been married four times now." He talked as he chewed the pistachios. "Alger tells me you're having a bit of a rough patch with your woman."

"That's none of your concern."

Donny ignored me. He jabbered about his first wife and the daughter they had together. "She didn't even include me on the birth certificate. I've been to court for this. I have no rights. A man has no rights." He tossed the bag of pistachios on the dash and pulled out a lockback and flipped it open. He rested his right foot on his left knee and started cutting the strands of worn thread from his pant cuffs.

"So don't get in too deep," Donny said. "Why are you with this woman anyway? Sounds like it's time you cut her loose."

"I don't know," I said. I was bullshitting him, I knew. Elise was better looking than anyone I had ever been with or ever would. I lost my virginity to some woman on the bathroom floor at party in West aka "Waste" Allis. I was sixteen and she was twenty-three and we smoked PCP before and after. I spent my twenties having one night stands with barflies I knew from the taverns around town, women ten years older than me who fucked me out of pity and nothing else. They knew I lived on canned chili and Hostess pies and worked in the tire shop at a cab company no one used because the cabbies boozed as they drove. Or I was living out of my Ford Taurus and working nights for an ex-con who collected unwanted wooden pallets and resold them to trucking companies. My longest relationship before Elise was with a girl named Daisy who worked the shoe counter at a twenty-four-hour bowling alley. I was working part-time at a sign shop for five bucks an hour and had nowhere to sleep. I would buy a single beer and drift off while some rerun played on the old television. Daisy never ratted me out and we ended up dating for six months. She left me for the security of a fifty-year-old guy who mixed paint full-time at a Home Depot and had a gambling problem.

Before Donny could start yammering again, the dispatcher's voice sounded from the radio. A contractor scab was stuck over on Kinnickinnic. I would have to cut through my neighborhood and past my apartment to go free the bastard. No one knew why the hell the city needed to contract these amateurs to help plow, these 1099s who usually cleared an insignificant residential street or two and stopped at the nearest tavern and called it a day. They were the kind of guys who had fuzzy, stuffed dice draped over their rearview mirrors.

The video dispatch appeared on my LCD screen. I hit go button before any of the other drivers in the area grabbed the job. "88. The scab's all you," the dispatcher said.

"She has a real nice voice," Donny said. "Very soft. I wouldn't mind meeting that one."

"It's a dude, actually," I said. "The dispatcher is a dude."

Donny thought about it for a moment. He took his bag of pistachios off the dash and used his long thumbnail to split the shell.

My phone buzzed again. *I am too tired to deal with your stress. You need to think about us . . .*

I wasn't one to respond to texts. I had to put in an hour or so just to compose one because I didn't understand the predictive text or any of that other shit that seemed to complicate the whole process. But I tried to respond to this one. I struggled to hit the buttons with one hand and steer the truck with the other.

"May I?" Donny asked, reaching for the phone.

"You may not," I said.

"I've learned the ladies like to text."

I didn't say anything more. I tossed the phone into the cup holder and turned onto Lincoln Ave. The street hadn't been cleared so I kept the blade down to guide me over to Kinnickinnic. But I didn't keep the snowplow at the maximum thirty. I hit the accelerator and brought the snowplow up to fifty. The blade chattered and the seams Chris had repaired threatened to split. The blade threw a wave of snow on the porches of the houses we passed.

"Hey, now," Donny said, bracing himself for impact. "Hey, now, buddy."

I blasted down Lincoln and took a hard turn onto Kinnickinnic. The plow blade caught a chunk of concrete and kicked it into a bakery's front door. If the owners complained, the union boss would have written me up for that one. Three snowfalls, three union violations. Pretty soon Donny would be in the driver's seat and I would be sorting batteries and computer chips in e-waste.

As I drove down Kinnickinnic, I saw the dishwasher's Civic parked in front of my building. The street was posted *no parking* during snowfall. I could have plowed him in, but I wanted the guy gone. I cruised around his lame little car and pulled into the gas station across from my building.

"I don't know what's going on," Donny said. "You're making me feel real uncomfortable, bud."

"Relax," I said. I reached in my pocket and pulled out a five. "Here. Go buy yourself more pistachios."

Donny looked over to the small twenty-four-hour convenience store. "My mom's been buying me these organic ones from Sendick's."

"You'll live," I said. Forty-five and still living with his mother. I almost felt sorry for the guy.

I cut the engine and climbed out of the cab. The bay window in the front of our apartment was lit up and I knew they were inside.

I wanted to tell Elise we were done, done, done. But I wanted to tell her she could stay at the apartment until she left if she wanted. I would relocate to the couch. I didn't want her going back to that flat with all those dish dogs.

Another plow cruised past and the driver honked his horn and flashed his lights. I waited for him to clear the street, the sludge to settle in the gutters, before I crossed the street. Donny called out to me from the gas station, but I didn't turn around to acknowledge him. He seemed like the kind of guy who would quit bothering you if you just ignored him enough.

I was right up near the walk when the dish dog poked his head of a window along the side of the house. He had a cigarette hanging from his lip. He evaluated the drop to the walk along the side of the house. I must have startled him because he let the cigarette go and dropped out of the window. He started toward the back gate, but his knee or ankle seemed to have twisted during the fall.

"No use, dude," I said, walking toward him. I pulled my keys out of my pocket and rattled them. "Gate is locked."

The guy stopped and turned to assess his options now that both ends of the narrow passage between the houses were blocked. He was wearing a Phish hoodie with a safety pin holding together a tear right in the gut. Really, Elise? I thought. Fucking Phish? Someone from his kitchen, the chef most likely, had probably tried to shank him during his shift. Most of my chef friends had uncontrollable tempers and cocaine habits.

Elise came to the open window. She was really worked up. She always caked on the mascara, so her face was streaked with black. "Oh, shit," she said. "It is not what you think about."

"I don't think anything," I said. I stood at the end of the passage. "I'm not going to do what you think I'm going to do." I could have ruined that guy, but he wasn't worth it. I liked to think my days of fistfights in narrow spaces were over.

"You two have shit to talk about. I'm out of here," the guy said. He put his hood over his head and started toward me. I noticed he had canvas Vans in Rasta colors just to top off the whole costume. He lit an American Spirit and took a big drag as he approached me. I took a step out of the way to let him pass, to have his little victory parade or whatever the hell it was he wanted. He should have just left, but he decided to ash his cigarette on me. Well, I thought, and hooked my foot around his and sent him to the pavement.

"Moose," Elise said. I turned and saw her moving past the windows toward the front door. She still had her chef's jacket on. She wasn't wearing shoes, but she walked outside anyway. "I do not want violence in this place."

"Yeah, man. Not cool," the guy said, collecting himself. He examined his Spirit for damage and dropped it on the ground.

Before I could go at him, Elise spoke. "We have a thing now we need to consider," she said. She said it softly, but it sounded louder than anything. There were reasons beyond drinking to explain her recent illness. She looked at the ground and ran her bare feet over the pebbles of ice melt.

The dish dog disappeared from the front lawn, him and his little car picked up and dropped somewhere far away.

Elise straightened up. She folded her arms across her body and hugged herself. "I cannot talk about anything with you." She went inside and closed the door.

I started to chase after her, but eased up. She didn't want to talk to me, not until my shift was over and the streets were clear. I would let her go inside and search around for the beer I'd taken out of the refrigerator. On a night like that, she would find it. She always did. In the morning, I would take the bottles off the coffee table in the living room and set them inside the recycling bin. I would stack the newspapers and magazines and recipe notes around the apartment. I wouldn't keep booze in the apartment anymore.

The strand of broken Christmas lights was sitting on the front stoop. She must have broken every bulb and cast them outside. I picked up the strand and dragged them over to the gas station. Donny had the passenger's side door of the snowplow open. He was eating sunflower seeds. He spit some shells into my coffee mug.

"No pistachios," he said. "But they had sunflowers seeds. Haven't had these since I was a child."

"You are a child, Donny," I said.

"Hey, now. That your lady over there, bucko?"

I turned and looked over to the apartment. The light in the living room went out. It took me a long time to answer him, but I finally did. "Sure is," I said.

He spit a wad of sunflower seed shells into my coffee mug and nodded. "Boy, oh, boy. She looks like she's really something."

"Take it easy, Donny," I said. I walked the strand of broken lights over to the pile of Christmas trees in the gas station lot. The tree attendant wasn't around yet, so I helped myself. I rifled through them and found a sad, sickly little one and hauled it out. I walked over to the hut where the attendant usually sat and shoved a twenty underneath the door. I'm many things, but I'm no thief.

I went back over to the tree and pushed the branches down to fill it out and dressed it with Elise's string of lights. A light came on again in the living room of the apartment. Elise stood in the window and watched me. I set the tree upright and approximated its width and its height. I didn't have space in the living room for a tree, but it didn't matter. I could make space. I could make space for anything.

Bee inside a Bullet

*C*ongrats, you snagged the one job in the East Bay that didn't require a resume during the application process. Before you left Milwaukee, the ex-hippie framebuilder who let you hang around his shop told you never to trust anyone who required a resume, which is why you spent the better part of your first month in California couch surfing at the apartments of friends of sort of friends and bumming around Telegraph during the day. You tried angel dust for the first time and went to heaven, but were glad when you got the call. The job's exactly what you wanted: knocking out the finishing work on bicycle frames. You have a three-frame-a-day quota, which is good because you don't trust things like W-2s and Social Security and taxes. You like to stay off the government's record.

You work in a small yurt behind Clay's Berkeley bungalow in the hills west of the Gourmet Ghetto. He shows you the stack of China-built frames that you have to braze rack mounts and cable stops onto. He tells you to clean up the sloppy brazing on the dropouts and lugs to make the frames look like they were built in Japan. He plans to tell customers the frames were built by a famous Japanese builder who has been previously reluctant to sell his frames in the

States. Clay shows you the jig you have to work with—a homemade job that he cobbled together with two-by-fours and whatever hardware he could find at the True Value. There's an alignment table too, but you're sure it's out of alignment itself.

When Clay retreats back to his bungalow, you stand there a moment and look at the pile of estate-sale brushes and files and other supplies. You note the short distance between the small workbench and the jig. You take the tape measure off the bench and draw the tape out to measure the diameter of the yurt you will be working in. The diameter measures eleven feet, so effectively you're working in an eight-by-eight shop because the yurt is round and nothing can be put against the walls. You're reminded of the tiny efficiency you rent with your new girlfriend and how she's excited you both may be able to move to a more suitable living situation now that you're employed and all.

She works in a psychology lab at UC Berkeley, the only job she could find after she graduated with a B.A. in French. She lied on her resume and said she was a Psych minor and they hired her as a low-level lab assistant. There's some professor up there doing experiments on bees and she's responsible for knocking them unconscious with ice and cramming them into bullet casings. She has been at the job for nearly a year and is starting to show signs of rather unconventional behaviors, behaviors unconventional to you at least, by bringing home small groups of committed polyamorists who close-talk you in the corners of your already cramped apartment.

"See, Rob, it's a lifestyle," they say. Last night there was one woman who tried to redirect the conversation to things less polyamorous and instead seemed very much interested in your new vocation.

"Fascinating. I'd like to hear more about it sometime," she said. She smiled and waited for you to respond, but instead you nodded and slipped away to the bathroom to drink one of the many expensive Danish beers they'd brought and listen for how many times your girlfriend laughed a little too hard.

When you heard them all leaving, you listened to her apologize for you. "He puts a lot of pressure on himself, but you can see why the emotional support just isn't there."

Later, you didn't bring up your general discomfort with polyamorists in close quarters. Now you're beginning to regret moving in with her after only knowing her a month, but that's the Bay Area way, apparently, because rent's two grand a month for a one-room dump with a hot plate for a kitchen. When she comes home alone at night, the good nights, she cooks you both a meal of something noodle-based on the hotplate and hums and rolls a bullet casing around her mouth while you watch the woman across the street do yoga in her front yard. And when dinner's over, you and your girlfriend climb into bed early and fuck and you fall asleep with the faint flavor of brass in your mouth.

You work your way through the tools and jigs to the small window on the yurt's door, the only source of natural light in the place. Across the yard, beyond the clusterfuck of sunflowers and mums and miscellaneous wildflowers, Clay sits in a weathered wicker chair, reading the paper. He sips an espresso from one of those little white cups that you see so many of the bo-bos around Berkeley drinking out of. You wonder if it tastes any better than the black coffee you buy every morning at the BP on Ashby. Your framebuilder friend in Milwaukee told you never to trust anyone who drinks anything but black coffee from a gas station. Clay pulls his hair back into a ponytail and pours himself another espresso out of an aluminum stove-top pot and you know he's a jackass and doesn't care if this framebuilding deal makes any money or not. He's one of the many Berkeley-style idlers you're starting to notice around town. They all have money, but no jobs and anyone from anywhere but here would wonder how these people have any kind of money. Old money, Goldrush or timber money, maybe.

You move back to the jig where Clay's set up the first frame you have to work on for the day. He's rigged a kind of fixture to hold the cable stops in place with vise grips and a few blocks of wood. He's already applied the flux and all so you're almost ready to go. You put the brazing goggles on and turn the gas on and spark the torch. He's laid out a bunch of old brazing rods of different sizes, none of them correct, so you pick up the one with the smallest gauge and turn to the jig. This is why you came to the Bay Area. You wonder what you'd look like to someone standing outside, say, staring through the yurt's little window. You think of the old-school image of Tom Ritchey that started this whole bike thing, your life always moving toward framebuilding. You think of how Tom Ritchey looked healthy and rustic and happy fillet brazing a road frame in his cottage-style workshop. How the years of framebuilding supplies hanging from the redwood rafters in the background made you, even at age ten, want to have a workshop crowded with such history. You wonder if you look like him standing in the yurt in your second-hand brazing goggles and frayed black t-shirt and torn jeans, waving the brazing torch around.

The yurt heats up in a hurry and you question how safe it is to be working in such a space. Dried redwood floors and frame, waxed canvas cover—the place wouldn't cut it with OSHA inspectors, that's for sure. You'll need to avoid your usual carelessness with the lit brazing torch, how you have a tendency to wave it around while working and in conversation. But no one will be visiting you, so the torch shouldn't be a problem. What if the place did go up? Clay wouldn't save you. He'd stand in his garden and take a few sips from his espresso cup and watch the place burn with you inside. You wouldn't know how to get out because the door is the only way out and it would be a flap of flaming fabric. Maybe you could cut your way out. You'll need to buy a good knife for such purposes and sharpen it regularly. Yes, Clay definitely wouldn't save you. He'd stay calm as he watched you, his business, burn. Maybe that's his plan—to wait until you burn the place down and find a way to collect the insurance money off the whole deal. Maybe he's done this before and that's why he doesn't really have to work.

You turn the torch off. You won't tell your girlfriend about your unsafe working conditions when you get home tonight. This sort of thing excites her, as do your stories about sleeping in Dumpsters and junked cars when you lived in Milwaukee, and she'll invite another group of polyamorists over, more eccentric ones who dress in pirate costumes in their leisure time, and ask you to tell them about your new job as they crowd around you. Instead, when she asks how your first day went you'll shrug and say work is work. You won't touch her lower back as usual when you pass her on your way to the sink, just to let her know it may be ending soon. You don't think she's capable of picking up on such clues anyway. You tend to do these subtle things when you're thinking about ending a relationship. You do them for yourself. She won't notice and instead will ask you if you are interested in a peanut butter and honey sandwich, which is your usual break from the noodles. She has this bee obsession now and has started using honey whenever it is even slightly appropriate. The sandwiches are her preferred means of honey intake. You know this because she pours the honey on. She sits at the little cafe table against the kitchen window and chews on the sandwich while telling you a bunch of random facts about bees. Like how they carry an electrostatic charge.

You know some unique facts now too, thanks to your new job. Clay gave you a comprehensive history of the yurt as part of the orientation process, complete with information about how yurts relate to his own cultural heritage. He told you that the word for yurt in Turkmen can mean "black house" or "white house," depending on the quality of the yurt. You asked him which his would be and he doesn't answer your question directly. "My yurt is top-shelf, custom built by my Turkish friends." Clay is half Turkish, his mother's side. He tells you that yurts were used by nomads in Central Asia, packed up and moved around, but his yurt is staying put.

You go back over to the window. Clay's smoking a joint and you make a mental note to search the garden for any roaches on your way out. Clay is the type of Berkeley lush who doesn't smoke his joints down, so you're hoping for an added bonus every day. Maybe he's doing you a favor because he knows you're in a tough spot and live in an apartment tinier than the yurt and have a bee-obsessed girlfriend with polyamorous interests and that she plans to take you with her into this opaque philosophy of love. Maybe he knows that you have a hard enough time showing affection for one person, let alone loving three. Maybe Clay's not that bad of a guy and that's why he didn't need a resume—he already knew you have lived in five states in two years and haven't held a job for more than three months. He already knew you prefer the neo-nomad lifestyle and always move in with girls who have at least one quality unattractive to you so you end up going through a tough breakup and have an excuse to relocate.

You could move. You could tough it out for a few weeks while you get everything organized. Your girlfriend wouldn't notice because she's too busy recruiting polyamorist groups to bring over to your apartment and convert you. You could bail, hitch a ride out to someplace less populated, like Wyoming, and find a job taking care of land owned by a guy like Clay. Maybe Clay has a friend with some land and a half dozen sheep and an A-frame cabin you can take care of for a few months. You could offer to make repairs to the roof of the A-frame. Ideally the place wouldn't have running water and you'd have to hike out to the well every morning to hand pump enough water for the day. You could start drinking tea, maybe even grow your own tea leaves. You could drink tea at night and look out at the sheep in the valley and decide they need to be moved because that's what shepherds do. But maybe one night you would notice the well water tastes faintly metallic and miss your Berkeley life after all. Just thinking about it now makes you miss it already and you haven't even left yet. You're learning to like honey, as it turns out, though your mother forbid you from such sweet substances throughout your childhood and you've always been terrified by the prospect of being stung by a bee again.

You walk back over to the torch and notice you've burned the better part of an hour just thinking about all this. Tonight your girlfriend will bring home another group of polyamorists for you to hide from. After work you'll steal Clay's roaches out of the garden and slip them into your pocket for later. You'll come home and introduce yourself to all the polyamorists and politely excuse yourself because you'd been working so hard at your new job that you neglected to use the restroom before you clocked out. You'll take one of the expensive beers and make a peanut butter and honey sandwich on your way. The bathroom window will be open and you'll be able to angle your head and watch the woman across the street stretch for a while. Then you'll sit in the empty bathtub and drink the beer and think about how things always taste better when you don't buy them and that's why you'll stay with your new girlfriend for just a while longer. You'll sit in the tub and listen to the muffled laughs and begin to understand how people may love more than one thing at once—bees, bikes, bullets.

Lifer

It happened to be up early checking on the screw jack underneath the house when Dutch jabbed my flank with the tip of his cane and told me to get a move on already. I brushed him off because I had felt the house drop during the night and was sure the cold had snapped the rod's threads. I nudged a cinderblock underneath a carrying beam so I wouldn't lose the corner of the house.

"Get your shit together," Dutch said. He had helped himself to the squirrel pelt hat my dead father wore when he went ice fishing. "Beverly does not tolerate the tardy."

Beverly was going to be my new boss, the woman responsible for straightening me out. The afternoon before I had liberated Dutch from the confines of the Lutheran Manor, an assisted living facility where residents received no assistance other than the occasional overcooked omelet or microzapped meatloaf. In exchange for my services, Dutch made a few phone calls and set me up with work at a wheelchair supplier in Milwaukee's South Side. Beverly had a wheelbuilder there, some dude named Quilt, who she said could teach me his trade. I would have the shittiest commute in Southeastern Wisconsin, at least an hour there and back going *with* the commuter rush, but Dutch said Beverly didn't bullshit on pay or cut employees from their shift, which was a whole lot more than I could say about any of the dirtbags I'd ever worked for.

"Is this going to be an every morning thing?" I said. "This six a.m. stuff?"

"Hell yes it is," Dutch said. "It's called being gainfully employed. There are places in the world where a man would call this the opportunity of a lifetime."

"Oh, you know me," I said. "I love an opportunity."

"Bullshit you do."

I was being a jackass, I realize. But I was interested in a career change. I'd spent the previous three months up at the family Christmas tree farm in Door County. I slept in a canned ham Aloha trailer with a gasoline generator that powered a coil heater and weak lightbulb. I ate Spam sandwiches grilled on the single-burner propane stove for every meal. I baled at least one hundred fraser firs and blue spruce for rich assholes from Chicago while they sang along to crappy Christmas music and waited inside their warm SUVs. And none of them slipped me a rolled up ten or twenty for my trouble. Not even once.

My uncle Gus was still off banging one of his barfly girlfriends in her trailer home so I was able to borrow Pop's Bonneville without Gus nagging me about it. Gus wouldn't have wanted me running up the mileage by commuting out to Milwaukee. Way he saw things, that Bonneville was a big chunk of his inheritance. He wanted that baby pristine. He would have to fight me over it though—Pop said the car was mine as soon as I had the cash to buy it outright. I'd been doing oil and filter changes on the thing since high school. When Pop bought new rubber for it, some genuine Goodyears, I installed them. Even though the Bonny was the stripped-down model, tape deck and manual door locks and cloth seats, the car was pretty much ideal. The body was as wide as a freeway lane, so drivers gave you plenty of space when they saw you coming up behind them.

The shocks were nice and worn and the Bonny floated right over uneven sections of pavement and potholes. The trunk was endless—you could spend the afternoon collecting scrap for profit and still have leftover space for a quarter barrel of PBR. And the bench seats in the front and back were broad enough for you to stretch out and sleep one off in a parking lot so you didn't have to risk a DUI. Shit, maybe Detroit wouldn't be such a wasteland if they started making vehicles like the '92 Bonneville again.

The low clouds had dumped snow at some point during the night and the plows were out in full force. I caught a WDOT gritter just before the on-ramp and settled in behind it. The driver dropped the plow and pushed the snow away clear out to the Milwaukee city limits. I kept the Bonneville in tight behind the truck even though the impeller was feeding salt and de-icer at a pretty good clip. The blue rocks of salt struck the hood and windshield, but I didn't back off. Pop's old Bonny was already covered with door dings and hail damage.

I cruised past Miller Park. The smokestacks of Menomonee Valley pumped steam into the air. I rolled down the window out of habit, but remembered the Red Star plant had closed a few years back. My mom always said you knew you were in the Valley when your nostrils filled with the stifling stench of yeast. That stench meant a good number of people had jobs and benefits and nice little icebox houses outside the city. Now all I smelled was the faint whiff of beer and discarded animal carcass from the slaughterhouse below the viaduct. I heard over one hundred people got the boot when the Red Star plant shuttered.

If you're going to pass through the industrial shit-storm that is the Valley, the yards of scrap and gravel, the parades of dump trucks piloted by unlicensed drunks, and venture into the Polish flats of the South Side, you better know where the hell you are going. Stop at a gas station and look around like some lost bumpkin and you're liable to get knifed and robbed. Lucky for me I'd done a couple dozen ride-alongs with Pop back when he would come down to the neighborhood junk lots to scout out crashers. We found the Bonneville down there, come to think of it.

I was late as hell, which was pretty normal for me. I saw the Basilica, the major marker on Dutch's directions, and gunned it around the corner. A school bus had slid and sideswiped a light pole but I scooted around it. Some women from a bakery chased after the guy I assumed was the driver. He ran out in front of me and disappeared into an alley. He knew he was screwed, his license gone, his job lost. Just add fleeing an accident to the charges. He was probably going to go straight to his favorite bar, nap against their door until they opened, and spend the rest of the day drinking away his last paycheck.

The wheelchair supplier was in an old vaudeville theater on the corner of the street. The street had shit for parking so I left the Bonny in a loading zone in front of a burned-out paint store. I figured the Bonny wouldn't be in the space long enough for me to get a ticket—this Beverly woman would take one look at my appearance and send me on my way. Besides, the pigs in that neighborhood had bigger problems than an illegal parking job.

The letters on the sign above the boarded-up ticket booth read BL CK WHEEL HAIR SU LY. The face of the building looked like someone had blasted it with a machine gun, which probably wasn't far from the truth. I had no idea what kind of freak show awaited me inside the theater. The Menomonee Valley had been crowded with tanneries and garbage crematories for all those years and word was the pollution had run off and permanently tainted the ground water on the South Side, which could have explained a lot about who and what I was about to find. But who the hell knew what was housed beyond the graffiti-caked exterior? I imagined being greeted by a man with a lone giant ear. Ushered inside by a woman balancing a folding chair on her head. A Cyclops flicking peanuts at a miniature elephant on stage.

The front doors to the theater were torn out and in their place were two rolling steel doors. Someone had pulled one of the doors wide open and no one appeared to be guarding the pallets dumped just inside the doorway. The face of the building bowed out over the door and seemed poised for collapse. The place looked like a sham, but I went inside anyway.

Some fat dude in a great stocking cap and Blind Melon T-shirt was sorting parts in what used to be the lobby. His gut hung down low and full like an udder and his pants had worked their way off his waist. He stood when he spotted me and hiked up his pants. "Something I can help you with?" he said. He picked up a loose two-by-four and tapped it against his palm.

"Yeah. I'm here to see Beverly Blick," I said. "She's supposed to give me a job."

The guy didn't move, didn't change his expression to show me any kind of recognition. I held up the scrap of paper where Dutch had scribbled directions so I looked like someone had sent me on official business.

"Around back," he said. "Her office is around back. We usually don't keep this door open."

I pointed to the maze of boxes. "Can I just cut through?"

"I said out back," the guy said. He threw the two-by-four on the ground and went back to sorting parts.

The guy struck me as the kind of asshole who meant what he said and I decided it would be best if I used the back entrance. I walked out front toward the side street and moved down the side of the building. A small liquor store was hidden in the side street. The front glass was encased in metal cages and High Life signs and the cashier inside was housed a glass case. The bullet-proof glass was so thick you could see only the shadow of him as he moved around the case. I figured I would have to sign over my first paycheck to buy a case of booze for Dutch, a proper way to thank someone who has landed you a job.

The alley had never been plowed, and I didn't want to get my boots wet, so I tight-roped along the frozen ridge of ice and concrete chips between the two tire tracks. A beater Mary Kay Caddy with salvage-yard doors blocked the alley behind the theater and I had to work my way around it to get to the back door of the theater. Nothing is worse than working a full shift in wet shitkickers.

The door on the backside of the building looked like someone had kicked it in, which apparently meant it was unlocked and Blick Wheelchair Supply was open for business. I pushed open the door and went on inside. A heavy woman in a Members Only jacket was sitting at a desk in the orchestra pit. She hunched over a mechanical adding machine. She brought the receipt ribbon tight and transferred the numbers to a ledger book. Her hair was gray and unevenly cropped like she had taken care of it with a set of pinking shears. I figured the woman was Beverly, so I started over there.

"No, no," she said. She didn't look up from her work. "Wipe your feet young man."

I went over to the water-logged doormat and kicked the salt rocks and street shit off my boots.

"Should have known Dutch would send me a boy with no manners," she said. "That's the problem with you people out in lake country. You are feral creatures."

She was right. I was lake trash, lake trash that couldn't afford to lose a job on account of lousy manners. "Yes, ma'am. I'm sorry," I said.

"Don't apologize," she said. She dropped the ribbon and set down her bifocals and swiveled to face me. "And don't 'ma'am' me. We aren't at no country club. Beverly is fine."

"Sounds good." I regretted throwing the "ma'am" in there. I'd never used the term in my life—it was a term best used by Southerners. In Wisconsin, if you respect someone, you look them right in their goddamn eyes and call them by their first name.

She leaned forward in her chair and sized me up. She could probably smell the stale closet on my shirt, the one I had pulled out of a box at the bottom of my father's closet. It was a real Dickies workshirt though. I didn't want to look like someone who didn't know how to throw stock or turn a wrench. But I was still wearing camoprint canvas boots—the only footwear I owned—like I'd just gotten done field-dressing a deer or milking a row of cows.

"Well, I'll have to fire some people to make space, but I think I can find a job for you," she said. "You have a trade?"

"I took some welding classes," I said, which was the truth. I'd taken a handful of courses right out of school, but ran into a surly instructor who wouldn't pass me on to the next level. He said the beads I made with the cold wire feeder looked like a farmer with a rod and torch had set them down. After I repeated the class and flunked a second time, I realized that I was an embarrassment to the family name and it was time to hang up my welder's mask. "Their classes helped me—"

Beverly cut me off. "Oh, no. No, no, no. I don't believe in classes. You want to learn a trade, you learn it on the ground. Only the unemployable teach trades at vocational schools. If they were any good, they would be pulling doubles and making real money."

A shotgun leaned inside the umbrella stand behind the desk. Beverly stood and shuffled over to the gun and grabbed its barrel. In a neighborhood like this, where the gangs would force their way into the building and hold everyone at gunpoint while they emptied the safe and raided the customer records for account numbers, it made sense that the owner walked the warehouse floor with a loaded weapon. I wondered if Dutch's story about Beverly's husband getting gunned down on this very warehouse floor wasn't made up after all. "Come on now, young man. I'll give you a tour and introduce you to Quilt. He builds wheels down in the cellar. If we're going to teach you a skill, you best learn it from him."

We moved through the rows of boxes packed with replacement tires and composite wheels and rubber grips. Beverly had ripped out all the seats from the theater and hauled them away, but the stubs of the floor-bolts still stuck up. I tripped over one and nearly bit it, but Beverly didn't say anything. She was too busy yakking about having the biggest inventory of wheelchair parts in the Midwest. Up in the balcony she had 10,000 replacement wheel bearings, the finest Swiss-made in the world. She said the damn things last a decade, but she thought she could do better, so China was shipping her a pallet of ceramics. "They say their bearings will outlive me," Beverly said. "But everyone knows that'll be damn near impossible."

A brake shoe struck me on the head and I looked up at the crumbling plaster ornament above. The employee who had rejected me earlier was hanging out on the catwalk, watching us through the hole where the theater's chandelier once dangled.

"Marshall. Dammit, boy." She was looking up through the hole at the guy too. "Don't you go sizing up the new employee. There's no need. He already has your job. Just punch out."

The guy stared at us for a few moments, then disappeared into the ceiling. I didn't like the idea of this Marshall dude launching aerial assaults on me every time I walked the floor, so I decided I'd make sure to take whatever bullshit this Quilt guy gave me in the basement.

"Marshall up there, Marshall's a special case," Beverly said. She gestured to the ceiling with the gun barrel. "He came to me through the city work program for addicts. They found him in a condemned tannery with a crack pipe hanging out of his mouth."

I nodded. I understood. My uncle Gus had demonstrated what

that shit will do to your life. He disappeared into Milwaukee for a few years, only to turn up fucked out of his mind in a gutted bottling house near the Pabst brewery. A group of volunteer social workers found Gus and some homeless woman curled up on a bed of Dumpster-picked clothes during a census of the bums. Gus and his girlfriend had been smoking rock out of a broken lightbulb. He took rehab over the pen in Waupun.

"He went from coke to crack in a year," Beverly said, shaking her head. I could tell Marshall wasn't the first half-recovered addict she'd helped. "Boy says the difference is like a revolver to a machine gun."

Flakes of plaster drifted down off the ceiling and landed on my shoulders and head. The phantom up in the rafters was moving away from us overhead. I could see the cracks in the ceiling widen and contract as he moved across the catwalk. An elaborate skeleton of wooden beams and braces held up one corner of the building, up in the balcony. The whole deal was a goddamn engineering master-piece, I have to say.

"Now I know what you're thinking," Beverly said. She must have seen me assessing the likelihood of the building's makeshift struc-tural elements failing. "You're worried that catwalk will come crash-ing down on your head. No need to worry. See those braces? I know the best brace-man in the city. He said the building will stay upright for generations."

———

Beverly assigned me to the wheelbuilding department, a single-man operation staffed by a guy named Quilt. The department was in the lower level of the basement, away from any chance of contact with a projectile, which suited me just fine. Yes, the basement had two levels and you got down there by taking an unlit staircase that wasn't any wider than a person's shoulders. The electrical system had apparently fried, so Beverly kept a few headlamps and flashlights on hooks beside the doorway. After you'd geared up, you would walk down the staircase and into the catacombs. The basement had a bunch of rooms where Beverly stashed piles of shit she'd bought on the cheap from bankrupt distributors and manufacturers, parts she claimed she could "eBay or whatever" for a good haul even though the woman had never turned on a computer.

Quilt's lair was down in one of the theater's decommissioned bathrooms that the actors had used. The ceiling hung low and a canopy of pipes and spider webs made sure you couldn't stand fully upright. Every twenty minutes or so, one of the pipes would hiss and expel a burst of steam that stank of raw metal. Quilt spent his days scooting around on a makeshift mechanic's rolling stool—he'd snapped the back off of a squat desk chair. He had cleared narrow pathways among the water-damaged boxes of spokes and nipples. Nothing was organized by size or gauge, but Quilt knew exactly where everything was. He'd worked down in that cave for nearly a decade and had never gotten around to labeling anything. He sure as hell didn't want an apprentice.

"See, I don't give a shit about nobody," he said a few hours after Beverly dumped me downstairs. He was loading a hub with spokes and I was trying my best to count and rubberband the spokes for the day's work orders. "Especially someone from upstairs."

I couldn't respond. My head was screwed. I had already knocked my head on the pipes several times and was trying to measure out some spokes down to the mil in the crappy light of the house-lamp down there. Seemed like every time I reached for a hub I would crack my skull on a pipe.

"Don't hit your head on that one, kid. That there is a gas line. Cast iron pipe. You'll be out a week if you catch it."

He dropped some linseed oil on the threads of a bundle of spokes. "I'll teach you my craft, but that don't mean you'll amount to anything. Beverly has tried to give me apprentices before, but she don't realize my work is a fine art. And you don't strike me as no artist."

I could feel a small egg forming on my brow from the pipe's blow to my head. "I'll try not to fuck up, Quilt," I said. "I don't like fucking up. I hope that's a good starting point."

"That don't matter," he said. He laced a wheel. He could load a hub and lace a wheel in under ten minutes. I tried to watch him as he worked, without him catching me. That was one of the rules down in Quilt's lair: don't fucking look at him. Beverly told me he had picked up the name Quilt after a near-fatal accident with a semi-truck. Before Quilt moved into a catacomb of the basement, he liked to ride his rickety ten-speed through the Valley to the warehouse every day. He was riding early one morning when a sleep-deprived truck driver from Missouri or Mississippi or some bullshit drifted into the shoulder and clipped Quilt. His foot caught on the rim and his body was yanked up into the wheelwell. The force severed his leg and shaved the skin off several areas of his body. When the paramedics unwedged what was left of him from the wheelwell, his leg was dangling by a thin strand of gristle. The paramedics hurled right there in the street, gathered themselves, and loaded him into the ambulance. The surgeons found a way to piece him back together, Frankenstein-style. He'd had some insane number of skin grafts, so the guys around the warehouse started calling him Quilt. He didn't really give a shit about the nickname and instead just lurked around the basement so everyone left him alone.

"You pick all my spokes and get the right rims rounded up and we'll show you how to lace a wheel," he said. "See, it's just like weaving a basket." He pulled one spoke over the other and pushed the threaded end through the rim eyelets. His skin pulled all sorts of funky directions as he worked the spokes. "Watch my hands, kid."

He looked up. "If you aren't going to watch my hands, you can go find yourself another task here."

"Sorry," I said, even though I really was watching his hands. I turned around and went back to measuring spokes.

"That's okay now. Hey, that's okay," he said. The clink of his work stopped. I heard the rollers slide across the floor, the release of air out of his chair. "Tell you what," he said. He was standing right next to me now. He stank like a public Laundromat. "Why don't you go fetch us some grub from the SuperAmerica. Ask Beverly for some dough. She'll front us a pair of fives from the cashbox."

———

I went upstairs and asked Beverly for the cash and she handed it to me without asking any questions. She didn't even drop her pen or stop recording numbers in the ledger. She just reached over to the cash box, unlatched the cover, and took out a ten spot for me.

"You'll take those off my time card," I said.

"You bet," she said. "I'm making you buy lunch for Quilt, so you'll be down a over an hour's wages."

I didn't argue. I didn't want to come off to Quilt as a disrespectful asshole. In fact, I wanted him to like me. The guy had already confided to me that his two favorite things in the world were sidearms and snack bars and that gave me an interest in keeping him happy. So as the newbie I would buy lunch from the SuperAmerica.

Marshall was up in the catwalk and plugged his fat face in the chandelier hole when he heard my voice. He made a gargling sound and moved his mouth around, probably preparing a nice wad of spit to fire at me when I passed underneath him. I used the back-door of the warehouse to avoid him. And I sure as hell didn't offer to get him anything.

The dining options on Burns Street were pretty lousy unless your stomach could digest pizza with a lake of grease over the cheese or a two-week-old rough fish pan-fried. As I moseyed down to the SuperAmerica, a dude tried to sell me some roasted chestnuts out of a cart. I thought that was ridiculous, a guy selling chestnuts, especially in this neighborhood, but I bought some anyway. The shells peeled right off and I ate them while the dude told me his goal was to move up to one of the busy carts by the ice-skating rink off the Lake. He ran a popsicle cart in the summer.

"I knocked up my girl, man," he said. "Twins. You believe that shit?"

I tipped him a buck and told him to take it easy. He didn't thank me. Instead he closed the lid on his cart and shoved it over the icy snowpack of the sidewalk, working his way back to the pickup point. He rang the cart's bells in some half-assed attempt to drum up a little business, but you could tell he was going to call it a day.

The SuperAmerica was the finest business on the block, all lit up with high-wattage fluorescents even in broad daylight. Wisconsin was dull and dark in the winter, but the franchise owners of this SA made the place seem like Florida in July. I ditched the rest of the chestnuts in one of the pots of dead flowers out front and went inside.

The winter-beaten attendant was trying to mop the floor, but mostly he was just pushing around a stew of dirty water, winter grit, and straw wrappers. He tried to corral the mess with a pair of those yellow caution signs with the cartoon guy landing on his ass, but the wastewater had run down the grout between the floor tiles and slicked the floor with black. I skated across the mess to the SuperFresh roller grill. The casing on the sad dogs was wrinkled and tough from weeks of rotating on the greasy rollers. I'd spent a good portion of my childhood subsisting on convenience store food, but I don't think I could have ever adjusted to regular lunches from the SA like Quilt had. He wanted two of these things, sausage and egg tornadoes, which were bone-dry from the heat lamp by then. I grabbed two and headed for the register.

The attendant dropped the mop right on the floor and the wooden handle slapped the tiles. He sighed and shuffled over the register. He was short and had a round belly and moved slow, but wore a great yellow beard to make up for it.

"Three nineteen," he said before he even reached the register.

I put the money on the counter. The attendant stopped to examine a cut on his index finger, licked it, and took the money. He tapped a couple of buttons on the register and the drawer popped open. Outside, a semi pulled into the pumps, slowed, then drove off.

"Trucker drove off with a tank full of Nordic Diesel this morning," the attendant said. "I knew he was going to do it too. Didn't come inside to take a leak or anything. I've tried to get the owners to make folks pre-pay. No one listens. I can always tell when I have a drive-off on my hands."

"You must have some experience with that sort of thing," I said.

"Been working filling stations going on forty-five years."

"Damn."

"Damn straight."

I thanked him and took Quilt's tornadoes and went back outside into the cold. The clouds were low and drifting across the city. A beam of sunlight slipped through a gap in the clouds. I still had six hours left on my shift, but Quilt had probably finished the work orders. When I got back to the theater with his lunch, I figured he would have me build some practice wheels and would check them after I left for the day. I would go home and curl up on my ratty davenport, not knowing if I'd done a shitty job, not knowing if I would be unwelcomed by Quilt the next day. And about the time I would drift off to sleep, Quilt would be unrolling out his sleeping bag and turning on his black and white Zenith. He would work the rabbit ears until the picture focused. Some people probably know they are lifers right away, from the first wheel built, the first floor mopped, the first fuel tank gauged. People like Quilt.

I walked back to the warehouse. Down the block, I saw the guy who had been selling chestnuts climb into the back of an Oldsmobile station wagon. He had dumped his cart in the gutter, one set of wheels rested on the sidewalk, the other in the street. A pile of chestnuts had fallen into the stew of slush and road grim in the street. He wouldn't be coming back for the cart. He was a deserter.

Quilt stepped out of the warehouse's front door. He squinted as his eyes adjusted to the muted sunlight. I figured he didn't ascend the stairs from the basement too often, especially during daylight. He held up his arms in frustration. "Got my lunch yet there, kid?"

"You need to trust," I said.

"I thought maybe you thought to hell with this job and run off at lunch."

"It's not that easy to get rid of me, Quilt. You better be ready to deal with me until I'm dead." I didn't want him thinking I was a quitter, someone unworthy of teaching. He looked at me a minute and tore into his tornado. I hadn't noticed how chapped and wounded his face was before. His lips were lined with the white of dead flesh, the rest of his skin red and full of small splits. I looked away and went back inside and down to the basement, where I would work and listen to the braces above me creak as the building slipped.

Polo

*C*hase has seen some top-notch polo players roll through the parking garage off Market, but none as good as Lou "the Legend" Brewer. Lou comes from some no-bullshit Rust Belt city—Chicago or Cleveland or Milwaukee—and is apparently a friend of Avi, the organizer of their underground Wednesday night games. Avi advertises Lou the Legend as the individual responsible for founding the urban polo scene in the Midwest, and his polo play shows. Lou can stop and swivel his bike ninety degrees, an effortless redirection, all while maintaining possession of the scuffed street hockey ball they play with. He can weave through the other players while bouncing the ball on the wide side of his mallet's head, tap the ball, and bat it through the construction cone goal posts. He can lift the ball high, loft it over the head of Big Tom, master of the track stand and San Francisco's best goalie.

Lou the Legend has a fuck-you attitude supported by a grizzly mountainman look, the same look of the drunks who had kicked Chase's ass when he was stupid enough to move up to Fairbanks. Lou plays polo fierce, teeth clenched, shoulders up, cranks always spinning. Between goals Chase sees him take swigs from a travel-sized bottle of Jack Daniel's that he keeps in his coat pocket. Chase can't find anything hipster or messenger about Lou: he doesn't have some big-ass messenger bag with seatbelt buckles or canvas stars or cityscapes or any of that custom shit everyone else at Wednesday night polo has. The anti-messenger, mechanic part of Chase appreciates the persona Lou has going, though Chase wouldn't admit this to any of the polo players in the Market garage. Chase is a wrench who just hangs around messengers as a job requirement and prefers black T-shirts and faded jeans and owns a solid color, pre-incorporation Timbuk2 messenger bag. Lou hauls around a weather-beaten Kelty pack, a 5,000-cubic-inch deal that looks to Chase entirely too heavy, complete with patches from damn near every national park in the country. And he plays with the thing strapped to his back. When Lou chases after a breakaway and the pots and pans inside the bag shift and clank against one another, Chase feels faint relief because he knows the guy won't be staying long. Lou swings his mallet and sends the ball neck-high at Big Tom. Tom ducks and falls to the garage floor. But afterward Lou doesn't shit-talk like Chase does, and Chase doesn't respect this. Instead he keeps his head down and circles back to the opposite baseline.

Chase doesn't like him.

"Fuck him," Chase says to Avi.

Avi laughs and ties his dreadlocks back with a faded bandanna. "The best. The best," he says. He offers Chase a tall can of Pabst, but Chase pushes away the warm can. Chase respects the whole union thing, but thinks Pabst has been reduced to the beer of Mission District hipsters and alcoholics worse than him.

"Pabst doesn't even make this stuff anymore. The brewery's been blown up," Chase says. He watches Lou pull the straps on his pack tight to bring it higher on his back. "I'm sure your boy can tell you that."

"You're a lush," Avi says. He swings his mallet against the sidewall of Chase's tire and pedals toward the baseline opposite Lou.

Chase looks at Amna, Avi's girlfriend he has spent the better part of a year scheming to steal away. Avi has picked up on his advances toward Amna, the way he tends to sit out the first game at Wednesday night polo to talk to her, the way he casually rotates his way to the seat next to her whenever they all meet up at the Revolution Café after polo. Maybe this is why Avi is putting up Lou the Legend for the week, just so Lou can take out Chase.

Avi and Amna are not the best match because, among other reasons, their names sound a little too alike and when Chase addresses one of them they both say, "What?" It's awkward for Chase and he has determined the whole situation would be resolved if she would just leave Avi for good. They're always breaking up anyway. That, and Chase has been a little down lately, starting to doubt his ability to be relationship-worthy. He has burned the better part of a decade working in shops and comes home every night reeking of tires and degreaser and has no 401(k) or health insurance or any of that other stuff responsible adults have. He wonders about the life he has chosen.

Amna smiles. "He's fun to watch."

Chase taps a brake lever and backpedals.

"I think they could use your help. You're going to play, right?"

She smiles again, but Chase doesn't answer. Dumpster Dave, one of the many poser messenger-mechanics who hang around the polo games, plays referee and tosses the ball into the middle of the court and everyone takes off after it. Lou moves ahead of his pack of teammates. He pilots his frosted pink Pinarello through the traffic jam at center court, swings his mallet, and strikes the ball free. Big Tom and Avi cross wheels in the confusion and endo, but Lou rolls on. His Pinarello's chromed seat stays sparkle in the garage's industrial fluorescence. He slows, levels his crankarms and pushes the ball underneath them. Ditch Weed Dan gives chase, but Lou steers left to the side of the ball and raises his mallet for the shot. Chase swears Lou cuts him a glance in the garage's safety mirror before bringing the mallet down on the ball.

Chase has had enough. He dismounts his bike and unshoulders his Timbuk2 and sets it against the wall. He pulls his mallets out of his bag and spins them to see which is least warped. He takes his Bridgestone XO-1 by the seat post and examines the left dropout. The XO-1 is his only functional bike and he needs it to ride to work at the shop the next day. That and the bike was gifted to him by his mentor-mechanic, Rick. The bike is the ultimate all-arounder— twenty-six-inch wheels, lugged frame and fork that accommodate fat mountain bike tires, old-school Mafac cantilevers, moustache bars with bar-con shifters. Rick and Chase took long rides up in the Oakland hills after work, stopping periodically for Rick's smoke breaks. But Rick smoked rollies for the better part of twenty years and had started coughing up blood on their evening rides. Six months later he was dead and his sister brought Chase the bike with a short note from him: "Shut up and ride."

Two weeks ago, Chase crashed the bike and is concerned the sloppy brazing of his repair won't hold much longer. Wednesday night is polo night, though, and he is riding R.I.P. Rick's XO-1 and Amna is watching and Avi is waving him onto the court.

A car honks somewhere down on Market. Lou rides figure eights behind the construction cone goal. He keeps his mallet up on the flats of his bars when he charges the ball at the play-in, but can drop the mallet to the ground and shuffle the ball away fast. Chase knows he will have to strike the ball away from Legend's shuffle and hope one of his teammates gains possession.

Chase rides over to Avi's end of the court to make the game seven on three. He doesn't want to be teammates with Lou, not that Midwesterner jackass. Avi shakes his head. "No, asshole. We're not a charity case. Join them. Even the teams out," he says.

"Piss off," Chase says. He retreats to Lou's side of the court, near the speed bump before the ramp to the sixth level of the garage. Chase doesn't much feel like playing after the funky leftover Indian food he had found earlier in the shop's compact refrigerator and then eaten for lunch, but his life has become small enough that he has to establish himself as the best player at Wednesday night polo. Lou takes a drink from his Gentleman Jack Jack Daniel's, a whiskey Chase has never been able to afford, but wishes he could. The whiskey would settle Chase's stomach. Lou's teammates, Chase included, watch him take down a good portion of the bottle. He doesn't offer any to the others. He caps the bottle and slips it back into his coat pocket.

Chase rolls up next to Rat Henderson, a Tulsa-born runaway living on skid row as a messenger, who is stationed away from Lou. "This is one fucked up sitch, man."

Lou does a track stand. "Jackass," Chase says. He hopes he says it loud enough for Lou to hear. He wants this guy off his polo court, out of his city.

"You're not the one who has been playing with the guy for an hour," Rat says.

Dumpster Dave walks to the center court and counts to three backward. Three. Two. One. He drops the ball and sprints off the court to the sideline where Amna watches.

Chase takes off early. He holds his mallet up on his handlebars like Legend and mashes the XO-1's pedals. The old Japanese steel of the frame bows and flexes. The spokes pop and settle. The bottom bracket creaks. He heads toward center court, converging on the same spot as Lou and knows he'll hit him if he doesn't pull back. But San Francisco is Chase's town—the fog, the dope, the punks, the polo—and he's not willing to share. He pulls the bars into his chest and stands up out of the saddle. He'll taco his front wheel if it comes to that.

When Chase hits Lou and flips over the bars, he feels Rick's old frame give out. Not a pop from the dropout breaking away from the frame, but a kind of slow tearing that ends when he and the bike hit the ground and bounce end over end. His shoulder and cheek drag against the abrasive concrete of the garage floor and bring him and Rick's XO-1 to a stop. He watches Lou split two defenders and tap the ball between the construction cones. Someone cheers and the voice echoes up and down the levels.

———

Chase doesn't like going over to Avi's rat's nest of a studio apartment, but Avi says he has a first aid kit, and Chase doesn't care to throw down money for his own. Avi disappears into the bathroom, and Chase moves himself from the Dumpster-picked couch in the living room area to a folding chair in the kitchen. He slides the chair against the window where he can keep an eye on Lou. Lou's down in the compost-pile backyard, setting up his tent. He doesn't put the rain fly over the tent, probably thinking because he's in California, he won't get wet, so Chase prays to the rain gods he doesn't believe in that they give him one of those February monsoons off the Pacific and drench this caveman motherfucker.

Avi comes out of the bathroom with a bottle of unlabeled hydrogen peroxide, duct tape, and a ratty towel. "Can't find the first aid kit, but we'll get you fixed up with this."

"Never mind," Chase says. He licks his finger and rubs some of the dried blood from his elbow, but it doesn't do much to clean the road rash. He takes the towel and peroxide from Avi anyway and starts to clean the wound.

"Your face is pretty trashed, man," Avi says.

Chase turns back to the window, this time looking into the window, not out of it, and sees the divot-like gash. "Jerk," he says.

"Want me to clean it?"

"I'll tell you what I want," Chase says. "I want you to go out into your yard and tell that asshole to pack up his shit and get out of my city."

"He's not that bad of a guy. Give him a chance." Avi walks over to the window and opens it. "Hey, Lou."

Lou stops organizing his tent stakes and looks up.

"Need anything?"

Lou shakes his head and turns back to the stakes. He has them all laid out in the one area of the yard with faint patches of grass. He works in the moonlight. The clouds off the Pacific are late.

The towel bloodied, Chase gives up on cleaning the wounds and tosses the towel onto the folding table. "I don't get it. That guy out there is batshit crazy."

"What do you mean?"

"Well, certainly you've noticed that he never talks, being his good friend and all."

Avi just shrugs, so Chase stands up from his chair. He's had enough. Rick's bike has been destroyed and he has no way of getting to the shop tomorrow morning. He'll need to cobble together a new ride by Sunday to be ready for the next round. He'll need to call in sick at work, maybe say he had a wreck and might have cracked his collarbone, say he could be out awhile. But Chase knows he should be honest. Rick never bullshitted anyone and that's why everyone, customers and mechanics both, respected him. Chase will tell the guys at the shop that he has to take a leave of polo, that they wouldn't understand.

———

Chase rides the 5 home and thinks about the bike he'll build when he gets to his rent-controlled efficiency. He figures he has a complete bike with a decade's worth of spare parts, mostly stolen from the shops he's been fired from, crowded into his apartment. He'll build up one of the bare frames hanging on the wall, probably the paint-stripped Fat Chance mountain frame he bought for fifty bucks at the Oakland Flea Market when he was living in the East Bay. He'll forgo derailleurs and shifters and the necessary cables and build it up as simply as possible. He'll use the pair of Schwinn cruiser bars he robbed off an abandoned bike in Golden Gate Park. He'll make the bike bomb-proof, polo-worthy.

When the 5-Fulton lets him off at the corner of McAllister and Lyon, Chase walks down Lyon and ducks into the small convenience store to buy a bottle of recession-friendly vodka. Chase plans to get piss-drunk and build the bike the right way on his Park home-mechanic work stand. He will fill an old Folger's can with cleaning solvent and take apart the old Shimano headset pressed into the frame and drop the bearing races into the solvent. He'll leave the races in the can until the solvent clouds black, then repack the headset with the Italian-import Campagnolo Lubrificante Grasso he has been saving for the right occasion, the right bike. He'll build the Fat Chance like Rick had shown him when he thought it was time Chase learned how to build bikes the right way.

"There are two ways to build a bike, kid: one way makes the shop money, one way makes the bike work," Rick said. Rick smoked his Bugler rollies and drank cheap Russian vodka from a cracked coffee mug and showed Chase the right way. "Never," he said, "and I repeat, never, use the grinding wheel to touch up newly cut housing." Rick worked the double-cut file against the housing's end. "You'll burn the inner liner all to hell and the cables won't run smooth."

He'll need to make a new mallet too. Lou plays with one of those fancy mail-order mallets with a genuine cane shaft and a custom grip, the type that all the middle-class techies who play in Golden Gate Park use. He will need some high-quality lead pipe to build his new mallet. He'll have to walk his hacksaw over to the tunnel by the Conservatory of Flowers where he has spotted a nice section of old drainage pipe. He'll cut off a healthy section and bolt it to an old ski pole. He'll pitch his current mallets with their brittle PVC heads. Instead he'll use his new mallet with the lead-pipe head, equipment banned from the Wednesday night games.

He stands outside the door to his apartment. He will build the new bike the right way, the way a legend like Rick would have.

———

He waits until he has polished off half the handle of vodka and strung the cables onto the Fat Chance before he heads out for the section of lead pipe. He switches out the carbon-only blade on his hacksaw for one suitable for cutting lead pipe and slips a spare into his coat pocket. The pipe will take two blades, at least, to saw through.

Outside, the roads are slicked with rain and he imagines Lou drenched and muddied in the compost stew of Avi's backyard, afraid to escape to the house through the muck of rotten apples and egg shells and avocadoes. He imagines Lou holding the unzipped tent flap open, looking out over the compost mudslide flowing toward him. He imagines Lou wanting in that moment to be back in the tundra of Milwaukee or wherever, away from the stink of West Coast progressives.

He takes Grove toward Golden Gate Park and hopes to avoid the beat cops that patrol the Panhandle. At four a.m. they'll be out there trolling for junkies and teenage runaways and miscellaneous loonies who loiter around the park. At this hour, he wouldn't last five minutes walking along the Panhandle, waving around a hacksaw. He doesn't have a record, though if someone were to see his bank account right now, they'd think he was some kind of ex-convict. When he steals this section of lead pipe from the City of San Francisco, he will commit his first real crime. Avi has been arrested several times for petty crimes—shoplifting organic pears from the produce market on Haight, slinging dime bags to suburban high schools kids outside Amoeba Records—and he wonders if Amna will like to hear the story of the materials he stole for his new mallet. Before Sunday night, he will have to add texture to his story for Amna, how he fought off addicts and bums in the tunnel, how he outran the cops.

He heads down to Hayes, runs across Stanyan, and then dips into the bushes of Golden Gate Park. He doesn't have a flashlight or cell phone or any kind of light, so he follows the network of hobo-built paths toward the Conservatory of Flowers. He tries to move through the gaps quickly, but the sandy dirt of the trails gives out under his feet. The dirt here is like the loose soil up in the Oakland hills where he went to dispose of the big Ziploc that contained Rick's ashes. When he went to spill the ashes over the rock outcrop, the rock and dirt under his foot gave way and he almost tumbled into the gorge with the bag of ashes in hand. He hasn't been back to the East Bay since.

The squatters rustle and turn in the bushes around him as he pushes his way through the park. He usually isn't interested in self-defense techniques and weaponry like one of those Dungeons and Dragons geeks, but tonight he is glad he has the hacksaw. Whenever he hears someone stirring in the bushes, he holds the hacksaw up like he's a person looking for an easy excuse to use the thing. He wonders if this is really deviant behavior for someone in Golden Gate Park this late, if his gestures actually intimidate anyone.

He reaches the clearing where the glass greenhouse of the Conservatory of Flowers stands. Across the flowerbeds on the lawn, the faint glow of the tunnel reveals a group of men throwing dice near the drainage pipe. Rick wouldn't approve of him stealing a section of the pipe, not because helping yourself to a section is illegal, but because Rick wouldn't have played some bullshit like bike polo in the first place. "A bike is for riding and exploring," Rick would say. "Not for fashion or anything other than that." Rick refused to help customers who even bordered on hipster and would instead send one of the part-time shop rats to help them. "Messengers and hipsters and all that crap—they never buy anything." Rick sipped his vodka. "Time toilets."

Rick and Chase were riding through Berkeley after work when he first saw a game of polo. "Garbage," Rick said. "Look at them riding around in little circles, chasing after a damn ball." Rick downshifted and pushed on the pedals. Chase followed. "Bicycles are for going places."

When they reached the turnoff to the doubletrack that led into the hills, Rick hacked into a handkerchief and turned to Chase. "Promise me you'll never sink so low as bike polo." He promised.

But after Rick peaced out on life, and Chase moved to San Francisco, he couldn't drum up enough motivation to go for a ride. He would put his ten hours in at the shop, then take the five home and drink and stare at Rick's XO-1 leaned against the wall. Polo was his attempt at getting back into bikes and so far the polo games twice a week have worked. He has gone polo low, but he doesn't care. Soon enough he will be strong enough to ride in the doubletrack of the Oakland hills again. He will be strong enough to manage the lung-buster climbs and not think about Rick.

He walks through the flowerbeds and toward the tunnel. The men look over to him. "Beat it," he says. He holds the hacksaw up in front of himself. He shows them how serious he is about the crime he will commit.

—

Sunday night draws a bigger crowd and all the players sit around trying to drink off their Saturday night hangovers. Chase cruises onto the fifth floor of the parking garage and someone hands him a bottle of Tecate and says, "Drink 'til you're sober!"

There's a warm-up game of three on four going on and Chase

sees that Avi is the player sidelined. Avi rests against a concrete post while Amna examines him, his pant leg shredded and bloodied.

Chase coasts over to him and jumps off the back of his Fat Chance. Part of Chase wants to school Avi in polo, but his real goal is to take out Lou the Legend. "What the hell happened to you?" he asks.

Avi doesn't say anything and instead rolls up the bloodied fabric of his tight jeans. "Lou," Amna says finally. She tries to straighten out Avi's leg, but he winces and pushes her off.

"Jackass," Chase says. He looks over to the court where Lou stalks a battle for a loose ball. The chrome part of his Pinarello flashes in the light, and Chase wonders if the bike means what the XO-1 did to him. Lou doesn't seem like the type to ride a frosted pink bike for the vintage appeal, so he assumes the bike was some kind of gift. He notices how clean Lou keeps the bike, that the chrome Campagnolo parts have been polished with great attention, that the white handlebar tape is fresh and evenly wrapped. Rick loved lugged Pinarellos. Whenever a customer would wheel one into the shop, Rick always took out the frame alignment gauge and called everyone in the shop over to the bike. "Half a millimeter. Alignment's perfect. I'd like to see some hack American builder do this." Chase admires the bike and wishes he didn't have to wreck the frame.

Lou flicks his mallet into the spokes of Rat Henderson's Bianchi Pista and sends him to the ground. He shuffles the ball away and heads for the goal. Chase doesn't need to watch the rest of the play and turns back to Avi. Brake squeal. No one cheers.

"I'm going to play in. I'll take your spot," Chase says. He pops the Tecate's bottle cap with a pedal wrench from his bag and hands the beer to Avi. "This will help with the bleeding," he says.

Avi holds up the bottle. "Where'd you learn to do that?" he asks.

"A wise old wrench once told me that a good mechanic can use any tool in his bag or on his bench to open a beer." Chase pulls his new mallet out of his bag. The fresh grip-tape sticks to his palm. He gives the homemade mallet a practice swing and can feel the lead pipe's weight on the end.

He takes off his helmet and tosses it onto his messenger bag. He won't need a helmet. Rick never rode with a helmet and instead covered his receding hairline with a dirty cycling cap pulled tight and low on his head. Chase is perspiring from the ride to the garage. He scratches the helmet-itch off his head with the end of the mallet. Lou must notice the new mallet because he laughs and take a swig from a bottle of Jack Daniel's.

Chase pedals to the baseline opposite Lou's. His teammates don't say anything; they've noticed the carefully built-up Fat Chance and already know what he'll do. They know, as Chase does, that Chase'll smash Lou the Legend's Gucci wooden mallet, then take out the spokes of his Pinarello's rear wheel. Chase'll recover the ball and race it to the construction cones. He'll score and circle back to find Lou in a heap of broken mallet and Pinarello. He will tap Lou with the lead pipe and tell him to get off his court.

Dumpster Dave drops the ball at center court. Chase starts pedaling, but something is wrong with his bike. He feels the left crank loosen, his heel keep falling to the ground at the bottom of the pedal stroke, the bike lift from the ground.

In the moment before he strikes the ground, he sees everything around him another way. He is back in the East Bay riding up Tunnel Road alongside Rick. His hands are Sahara-dry from the sandy Zep hand cleaner in the bathroom at Studio Bicycles in Berkeley. He sweats out the smells of the shop—citrus degreaser, fresh tires, cardboard. They crest the hill above Oakland, and Chase turns back to look at the lights of the Bay Bridge, the bungalow houses, the Oakland docks. Rick lights a cigarette, as always, as they coast along the flat section of road. He coughs. They don't speak. They ride in the dirt of the wide shoulder until they reach the split-rail fence where Chase likes to stop and look down on all this.

Wake

Builders said my uncle Mack could see shapes in the trees, and that was the honest-to-God difference between the two of us. They sat around folding tables at the V.F.W. Post after the memorial, pulled on their Pabsts, and said the bastard could see a skiff's-worth of lumber in a downed horn timber. I knew Mack was better than me, though, and I sure as hell didn't need them telling me what kind of sawyer I was. I had started working the other side of the sawmill in my uncle's yard when I was twelve and stout enough to push the length of the logs through the saw. I spent fifteen years as my uncle's sawyer apprentice—his apprentice, that's what Mack had always called me. Mack had drilled me to locate keels and knees and stems in large timbers. He would walk a lap around a downed timber and test me on cutting strategies until my answer aligned with what he saw. I never got it right on the first try.

"Wouldn't use anyone else's planking," a builder told me as he stumbled to his pickup in the parking lot. "That's no bullshit."

The tip of the man's left index finger had been sheared off, I remembered later as I looked at another postcard from him. The front of the card had a photograph of Brett Favre, his chin strap unbuckled and flailing in the winter wind of Lambeau, hurling a pass. The note on the back was simple: "I give up already. Sawing yet? I need boards." I stuffed the card back inside the mailbox with the others. The polite thing would have been to send the man, and all the other builders, a proper response. I should have sat down and penned a letter to them on the leftover Schott Marine Timber stationery from Mack's bureau. I should have told them I couldn't deliver lumber. But sometimes, when I was working on the saw-mill's busted engine, I thought I could see the shapes as Mack had showed me. The shapes would emerge in flashes of remembered timber. That breasthook on the blow-down up in Brule River. That transom on the lone pine felled in the meadow beside the rail line. But I could never quite hold the shapes.

I would have liked to have settled in and waited, spent my days sitting on a stool in the yard until the shapes started to appear again, but I was one of the few year-rounders lucky enough to snag a gig at Merritt Boat Supply, all eight-fifty an hour. Merritt was the only marine store, marine anything, around Oconomowoc that had enough cash flow to take me on. Mack's bills were still showing up in the mail in rubber-banded bundles and I thought I might like to pay those off before the bank people came around to haul away the sawmill and timber crane. Chuck Merritt had even promised he would show me how to rebuild inboards during the winter, so I'd already decided to sit out sawing season.

I pushed through the switchgrass and into the yard beside the storehouse. The sawmill's tarp, a miserable, woven plastic thing that shed blue splinters, a replacement for the fitted canvas one, had lifted off the sawmill and caught on the branches reaching out from a leftover stump. Mack had sawed almost a whole yacht's structural elements from that one tree, a massive white pine we trailered all the way from the Minnesota border. We beat a part-time sawyer from the Twin Cities—a real hack who couldn't saw around knots and sold lousy boards out of his home's carport—to the tree and milled the lumber for a restoration job the owner had shelved for three years. The owner of the crippled yacht paid us twice the going rate for the lumber, so we took some time off and spent the spring and summer building and racing a pair of lapstrake double-ender dinghies. We chased breakaways in the races, placed a few times. Afterwards we drank Hefeweizen out of a glass boot at the biergarten in town.

The tarp's aluminum grommets were snagged on the tree's dried roots, and I ended up tearing it while trying to free it. I had already patched a long tear with duct tape a few weeks before. It couldn't handle another repair, so I would have to discount my time card at Merritt's a fresh one. I shook off the rainwater and tried to fold the miserable thing, but it wouldn't stay flat because of my shoddy patchwork. Mack would have kicked me square in the gut if he saw me using one of those blue tarps from K-Mart, or anything bought at K-Mart for that matter. He would have expected me to go into his workshop and fetch some fishing line to stitch the tear in the canvas one. "Don't you ever go buying tools there," Mack said one time as we passed the dim light of the K-Mart sign. "Ron Stephens shops there and that should tell you pretty much all you need to know." Ron's son had broken both bones in his forearm when the sketchy tree house Ron built collapsed. I was playing ball in the next yard over and saw the kid's crooked arm, the blood dripping to the dirt, the cracked bones pushed up and out of the boy's skin.

I brought the lock pick out of my back pocket and started working the storehouse's Master Lock. Mack had rented the yard and storehouse from the neighbor, old man Hamer, for thirty years. The key to the lock had been missing in the lake's muck for fifteen. The first lesson Mack taught me after my mom dumped me in his yard and disappeared forever was how to pick that lock, how to listen for the click and feel for the release.

Something stirred in the grass behind me. I'd caught feral cats in the yard twice before, cats looking to set up shop in the low crawlspace underneath the storehouse. But the creature wasn't a cat. It was Zeus, George Hamer's elderly Chesapeake. Zeus, chest stretched into a sack of fatty tumors, lumbered across the yard's limestone gravel. Mack called Zeus king of the lake, keeper of the ducks and cats around the yard, before Zeus went blind and my uncle began to wheeze. After Zeus walked off the end of our winter-buckled pier, George's wife begged him to put down Zeus, but George was a stubborn son of a bitch who needed a dog to match him. "Dog can still swim," he told his wife. "When he can't swim, I'll know it's time."

Zeus let out a low huff, so I went to him. I grabbed the bandanna around his neck and guided him to the tin of biscuits Mack kept outside the storehouse. I'd reloaded the tin several times and had given the Chesapeake as many biscuits as he was willing to gnaw even though George blamed the dog's weight gain on me. "Here, boy," I said, lowering a biscuit to Zeus. He clamped it with his front teeth and pulled it from my hand. He lowered himself to the pad of sawdust swept against the storehouse's corrugated side and began working his jaw to break apart the biscuit.

"You better not be feeding that dog," George said across the yard. He cradled a cocktail glass of brandy old-fashioned in his left hand. When he stepped onto the bridge spanning the banks of the narrow canal that divided the yards, the planks creaked under his weight. He gimped across, bum knee still stiff from a fall while ice fishing the previous winter. George Hamer was a tough old bird and he didn't much care for doctors, nurses, or hospitals. His knee had been busted since winter and the elastic brace he bought at Walgreens hadn't done a thing. Tough as he was, he didn't like coming across the bridge, so I knew what he wanted. I'd put him off for six months, and we still hadn't settled up on the rent for Mack's yard.

George reached the bridge's centermost point, and the planks bowed, but the supports stayed rigid. Mack built that bridge with two telephone poles rescued from a railroad lumberyard. Even though the name of his business made his purpose clear, folks would still phone for reclaimed railroad ties and telephone poles, so he liked to keep a healthy inventory of both in case the opportunity for a quick buck presented itself.

Zeus sniffed around the sawdust for crumbs, then rolled onto his side. Whenever we used to saw, Zeus would come bounding over the telephone pole bridge and roll himself in the fresh shavings and steal a biscuit from the tin. "Dog's so damn smart he can open the lid," Mack would say as the sawmill's engine wound down.

George cut through the path worn into the tall grass and stepped into the yard. A loose floorboard almost tripped him up and he splashed some of his old-fashioned onto me. Ever since the Schlitz brewery shut down, George had been nursing old-fashioneds. He fit pipes at Schlitz for thirty-five years. The day George and the rest of the crew were pink-slipped, he finished off the Schlitz in his refrigerator and started with the old-fashioneds. He came into the yard, rolled up his sleeve, and caught me by the shirt collar. I looked at the Schlitz tattoo bled out into his forearm's flesh. "Don't you ever forget who brewed your beer," George said. He tightened his grip on my collar and gave me a shake. "And don't let me catch you drinking anything but."

George hobbled over and slapped my bicep. "Starting early today?" I asked.

He raised his glass and a wave of amber rose over the rim and curled back into the glass. "You always were a lightweight, Russ," he said.

I held my tongue. Okay, I'll take it, I thought. You can't go mouthing off to someone you owe money, especially not a man like George. He saw a whole pile of money in the yard, from the uncut timber to the loose boards on the ground. Friend of Mack or no, he would have sold my stock and bulldozed the storehouse if I wasn't careful. The yard was about the only source of income he still had.

Besides, I didn't know who my father was and by then I didn't care much. My mother was restless when she was young, apparently, and had become some sort of addict. She surrendered me to my uncle when I was twelve and old enough to work in the yard. Last I had heard she was living in New Mexico and working on an ostrich farm. Some boozer at Sidearm's, a truck driver who lived in a house trailer on the outskirts of town, claimed he hooked up with her every now and then, said he would drive down there and they'd get loose on Jack Daniel's and she'd cook him ostrich steaks. "That meat—eating those dry old birds is pretty rough, kid," he said to me one afternoon. "Let me tell you. Be glad she didn't haul your ass down there with her." Later, I thought about breaking a pool cue over the man's back as he struggled to relieve himself in the bar's lone bathroom. I imagined stabbing the jerk with the splintered end of the cue. But when I walked into the bathroom, he was slumped against the urinal divider. He mumbled something and slid to the beer-soaked floor. Didn't seem right injuring a man that trashed, scum or not. I didn't have it in me anyway.

George pushed around some loose wedges and carlins and floors. The hoodlums around town had been poaching boards from the yard, but the only boards left were discards or bad cuts. I took up a board and gave George a jab in the ribs. "You have a blood stain on the front of that shirt," I said. "And you wonder why your wife can't stand the sight of you."

"You're low, just like your uncle," George said. He took a sip of the old-fashioned and fished one of the maraschino cherries out of the glass. He bounced it in his palm and popped it into his mouth. "Your buddy Champ showed up last week. Borrowed the twenty-eight-inch saw."

"He break into the storehouse?"

"Little bastard can pick a lock."

I let it pass. I knew Champ was hard up for money, but the kid wasn't foolish enough to pawn the saw. Champ was raised on the townie-trash shoreline across the lake. He learned how to swim in the silt-bottomed shallows of Muck Bay, keep the roof from leaking by slopping on layers of hot tar each summer, level his house with a hand jack and some cinder blocks. He'd lost both his parents— mother to drowning, father to drunken car wreck—by seventeen. Before Mack fell ill, he took Champ onto our summer crew. The shotgun crew, a group of anemic teenagers from the river bottoms on the outskirts of town and college kids looking for some extra beer money, handled most of our ugly summer jobs, breaking down thunderstorm blow-downs and rotted willows for folks who could afford a service. Most of the species weren't good enough for marine timber, so Mack and I supervised and did little else on these jobs. Tree removal wasn't sawing, wasn't real work. It was just one of the things that kept us alive during the summer.

"Say, Dave Reinhardt came around asking about the double-ender," George said.

"Not for sale," I said. I tossed a ledge onto the stack of weathered discards. The yard's rent payment was only a couple hundred dollars, but I hadn't paid George in six months, not with Mack's bills continuing to roll in. He had been eyeing the racer—a lightweight dinghy Mack built with no regard for expense. The boat could sell for far more than the delinquent rent, but I wasn't about to hock it to some rich lawyer like Reinhardt. I had watched Mack outsail Reinhardt during Sunday races too many times to let Reinhardt race Mack's boat.

George kicked one of the unmilled timbers in the yard. "You going to start sawing again? I saw the letters in the mailbox. Builders want your lumber."

"They don't want my lumber," I said to quiet him. A whole pile of my screw-ups sat stacked along the storehouse. Every tree in the world would have to be felled before a builder would have considered using even a single board. Whenever builders would visit our yard, Mack would always throw an old blanket over the boards to cover the disasters.

George pulled the long hairs on his eyebrow, and took an extended pull to finish off the old-fashioned. "I say you mill some of these here trees. Trees don't keep forever."

"They'll keep," I said. "Treated the ends with Anchorseal." But I was overselling him. Despite my efforts to stall weather's advance, the Anchorseal wouldn't hold the wood for much longer. The longer I waited for the shapes to come back, the more the wood checked and dried, the more the life went out of it.

———

George used a pair of needle-nose pliers to work the treble hook out of Zeus's paw. "Damn fishermen casting into the brush along shore. Found dozens of broken lines this year," he said. Zeus pulled his paw toward the bag of tumor below his chest. "Easy, boy. Hold him still, Russ."

I gripped Zeus's upper leg, and George twisted the pliers. Zeus tensed, but didn't whimper. A wasp had stung him on the same paw when he was a pup and he held still while George extracted the stinger. He was a hell of a dog, holding on through hairline fractures and failed eyesight. I scratched behind his ear.

"Sailboat race tomorrow," George said. He freed one of the hooks and set to work on the other. Zeus flinched. He knocked over the old-fashioned and the cloudy drink spilled into the lawn. "Hey, now. Hey," he said to Zeus. He rubbed his belly to settle him. "Anyway, I'm thinking it might be good for you to get back out on the lake once. Especially if you're not going to sell that boat."

"I don't race anymore," I said. Zeus shook his leg, so I tightened my grip.

"Suit yourself. I'm taking the Sanpan out for a cruise during the race. I'll take you along if you'd like."

"Not until you fix those rotten floorboards." He had owned the Sanpan since he bought the property—in fact, the previous owner threw in the pontoon boat as a bonus when George bought the place—and the floorboards were completely soft. A few years before, he replaced the deck, but did it on the cheap. He bought some strand board at True Value after refusing Mack's offer of the overstock marine plywood we had in the storehouse. After that, Mack wouldn't let anyone ride on the pontoon. "You'll fall through the floor and get mangled in the propeller," he said to anyone who got anywhere near the Sanpan. "That boat is a death trap."

George freed the final hook from Zeus's paw and wrapped a clean shop rag around the wound. He secured the rag with a strip of duct tape and patted the dog's flank. "Off you go, boy." Zeus stood and limped back toward the house, keeping weight off the injured paw. Mrs. Hamer leaned against the doorframe and watched with her arms folded.

I waved, turned to George. "He still running into the sliding glass door and furniture?" I asked.

"Some. Dog finds a way around. He can still see the outlines of things."

I looked down the shoreline and saw the Anderson twins out on the end of their pier. They swung around the last summer sparklers and dangled their feet just above the water. They waited for their father and mother to sweep across the bay, father behind the wheel of the restored Chris-Craft barrelback, mother on slalom ski in tow. Cass Anderson was still the best slalom skier on the lake, had been since she was a girl.

The boom of the Chris-Craft sounded across the lake, and Paul Anderson steered the boat into the bay. Cass, wearing cut-off jean shorts and a black bikini top like always, slalomed behind the boat on her vintage Gull Toothpick. She had bought the ski from Mack. He liked to comb barn sales for antique waterskis to restore. The restoration jobs were easy summer projects that he would palm off on me and then auction the skis for a healthy sum after I refinished them. It seemed he had bought up every classic ski in a fifty-mile radius because I hadn't been able to find one after he passed.

Cass cut across the wake and drove up an arc of water behind her. As the boat cruised past her girls, she hooked the handle into the crook of her arm and gave her girls a wave.

"Some things don't get old," George said.

"Beautiful boat," I said.

"I was talking about the girl, jackass."

"Right. Right," I said.

I had spent my childhood watching that boat cruise past the sawmill's yard. I finally convinced Paul to take me out for a ride a few summers back after Mack milled some replacement boards for the boat. When I delivered the lumber, I played it like I'd milled the boards myself so Paul couldn't say *no* to my request. I sat in the jumpseat while Paul drank a martini and drove and Cass slalomed behind the boat. The Chris-Craft's heavy body, unlike modern fiberglass speedboats, could cut through another boat's strong wake on days when the lake had heavy traffic. This is lust, I thought as I listened to the roar of the inboard engine. After Paul was good and liquored up and I begged him, he let me take the wheel for one lap around the lake, but we didn't make it even halfway before Paul forced his way back into the driver's seat. He had lived on Lac La Belle for ten years, but still hadn't learned the lake's shallows. The threat of a pierced hull or bent propeller made him skittish.

"Remember when Mack and me took you to the Fowler show?" George said.

"Sure do."

"The skiers made you dizzy. You puked up cotton candy on my shoes that one time. Had to pitch my best pair of sneakers thanks to that weak stomach of yours."

"I'm sure it wasn't a big loss. You've always worn the rattiest tennis shoes in town."

Cass spent her twenties as the main act of the Friday night ski show on Fowler. Every Friday Mack and I had the same routine: we would pile into Mack's Cutlass convertible, go to a fish fry at one of the churches in town to load up on beer-battered cod, potato pancakes, and dark rye, then walk over to the pontoon piers to watch Cass. Out-of-towners said she was the smoothest slalom skier they'd ever seen, that our little town was lucky to have such a talent. She would make the men sweat, the women frown. She would splash the crowd with her ski's rooster tail as she passed. That always made everyone applaud. Oconomowoc lost the big draw of the show when Cass settled down, married Paul, and had the girls. Several churches shut down their fish fries, kids started getting into more trouble, a few restaurants shuttered.

The Chris-Craft passed the pier again and Cass let go of the tow rope and glided toward the end of the pier. She ditched the ski and fell into the water. When she resurfaced a moment later, her daughters laughed and shook the sparklers until the lights went out.

"Real nice family they ended up with over there," George said. "Kind of makes your uncle's yard look like an eyesore."

I followed the Chris-Craft as it curved back into the big section of the lake. The engine continued its finely tuned roar, the kind of sound that could convince someone it would run forever.

—

George had mixed a serious old-fashioned, a Sunday morning old-fashioned, in a thirty-ounce thermal mug from Kwik Trip. He leaned back in his captain's chair and swiveled to face the lake. Through the tall grass on the shoreline, I noticed the regatta had already started and a breakaway had emerged. I squinted to see the numbers on the sails, but couldn't tell who was in the lead without my glasses. The hinge of my glasses had been broken going on a year, and my eyes were about as useless as it gets. Sometimes I wished I had full insurance, that the option of a union job on a manufacturing line in Milwaukee hadn't dried up when industry failed. I could have settled down as a machinist or welder, earned a paycheck and a pension. But those jobs were long gone, the laborers reduced to drinking old-fashioneds out of free travel mugs on Sunday mornings.

"George," I called.

He swiveled back toward the shore. "Russ. No work for the lazy man today?"

"Day off," I said.

He stood and held out his arms. "Then you've come for a cruise on the finest sea vessel on La Belle."

"Not quite. Not on that boat anyway. I was hoping for a tow." I tapped the toe of my boot against the beached racer's hull. I pulled the canvas tarp off the boat and pushed the mast upright, just in case I needed to cut the towline and sail back home. With George, I always had to be ready for him to lose it.

"Sure thing, kid," he said.

As I prepped the racer, I fought off the pull of guilt back the Merritt Marine. Tommy took the day off on Sundays so he could attend First Lutheran, which left me to run the store solo. But the store wasn't open that Sunday; I had deserted it without leaving an explanation on the door. When I left, I started to write a note to tape to the door— "Will return this afternoon"—but stopped when I realized I wouldn't.

The engine on the sawmill was still busted, but I knew I could get it running by sawing season. Champ was anxious to saw real lumber, and I could take him on as an assistant for deferred pay. Until then, there were still two, three good sailing weekends left. I'd sold enough twelve-pound anchors to condescending rich kids with modern ski boats, resold the same type of anchor to them the following day after they failed to tie a proper knot. Oil grades bored me, and I'd given enough explanations to recreational customers who questioned my expertise anyway. I'd grown tired of referring them to the perfect-bound oil guide chained to the end of the aisle so they could verify what I'd just recommended.

"Looks like there's a breakaway already," George said. He sipped the old-fashioned and took his boat keys out of his shirt pocket and turned the ignition. The ancient Evinrude sputtered, but he adjusted the choke and the engine idled properly. He released the bungee cords securing the Sanpan to the pier and put the engine in reverse.

The air choked with the Evinrude's exhaust and its blue smoke crept over the lake's surface. The Evinrude didn't have many trips on the lake left in it, but it had enough to carry my racer out of the bay. I spun a line above my head like a lasso and threw it out to George. Most sailors would have thought I'd become lazy for taking a tow out to the wide part of the lake, but I could still catch the flow of the race, sail alongside the fastest wealthy kids and their fiberglass dinghies.

George nudged the throttle forward and the Evinrude let out a high-pitched scream, a sign it was suffering its last. Even though the engine cried, he pushed the throttle and the racer's bow lifted and leveled. I'd forgotten how twitchy the racer could be when not loaded with gear. Mack built the boat according to a Scottish designer's rigid materials specification of lightweight marine plywood.

I watched the yard as the pontoon carried away my boat. The blue tarp had blown off the white pine timber, the curved timber we trailered into the yard a month before Mack passed. We had taken an order and payment for a pile of transoms from that log, but we never delivered. As Mack held on, he told me what the yield should be, and I agreed even though I couldn't see how to make the cuts and never would.

The weathered cordage I used as a towline threatened to snap, so I slid to the bow and untied the towline to release from George's pontoon. I pulled the halyard to raise the sail. The sail caught the wind, the boat heeled and steadied enough that I could exit the calm water between the pontoon's wake. I adjusted the sail and turned the tiller and cut through the wake. The racer picked up speed and the yard moved away quickly. For a moment, I thought I saw the silhouette of a man lumbering across the yard. He went up to the white pine timber and patted the bark. He pulled off his work gloves and ran his bare palm the length of timber. He could see the shapes.

No one was in the yard though. I saw the outline of the long trunk of timber beside the storehouse and the switchgrass shifting in the breeze. But I felt if I just looked long enough, I would see Mack out there in the yard, gloved and goggled, readying the saw to make its next cut.

Telegraph

*T*he first thing Dave tells Eagle is that under no circumstances is he to go near his office. Dave's office is a walled-off square in the back corner of the dark storeroom at Med Mart, the shady medical supply off Oakland's Telegraph Avenue. Dave keeps the door to his office secured with two key-operated Master Locks and an industrial-quality deadbolt. He has been here fifteen years, since the beginning when Eagle's uncle decided the rich folks in the Oakland Hills were on the decline and the area was primed for a medical supply store. Dave intends never to fall victim to an armed robbery.

Dave sucks on a raw sugar cane from the Vietnamese grocery down the block and says through darkened teeth that he can tell Eagle has never been involved in a live robbery. "You may have been able to survive in those woods," he says. "But this isn't some camping trip. You're in Oakland now. This is the real deal. Bear spray don't work here." He sets his sugar cane down on a wax-paper plate and reaches underneath the counter and produces an aluminum Easton baseball bat. The grip-tape has been replaced with white athletic tape from the display rack near the door, what Eagle takes to be Dave's invitation to petty criminals, adolescent shoplifters and such, taunting them to try to rip off something from his store. Eagle holds the bat and looks for vestiges of bodily harm—blood, bone, gristle, hair—but finds none. He hands the bat back to Dave and Dave snatches it from him and takes a practice swing.

"Never worked with another person, never wanted to, but your uncle has forced you on me. So I have to change my plan. You and this here bat will be the first line of defense," he says.

Eagle doesn't want to use the bat during a live robbery and he no longer wants this job at Med Mart. He wants his old life as a contract trail-builder back, but none of the conservation companies will dare hire him after rumors hit the listservs that employees of Other Mountain Conservation, his former employer, helped themselves to a significant number of tools and equipment. The bigger contractors he wants to work for have figured out that leadership at Other Mountain instructed younger trail-builders-turned-grant-writers like Eagle to write bloated supplemental proposals for government funds, and they may have skimmed some of those funds or purchased certain equipment that employees simply kept after the contract expired. Everyone was doing it, leadership said, asking the federal government for a little more cash than necessary, and so they told him to exercise exactly zero restraint when writing grant proposals. He wanted in at one of the high-visibility outfits, groups featured on Discovery and CNN and such, and so put those four years of liberal arts education at Saint Mary's College to work and authored long-winded, hellaciously complex grant proposals that most government contract specialists would approve without even attempting to read. "You're going places in conservation," his boss said. "No doubt."

He has sent out a few feelers to certain questionable friends in the business, but even they won't take him onto their ragtag crews as a grunt, a dirt-mover or shovel-cleaner. And so he lost his sublet in San Francisco and his Pontiac Vibe with custom roof rack and was forced to cheaper rent and shit jobs across the bay in Oakland.

In exchange for six days a week as a sales-associate-slash-stock-boy at Med Mart, his uncle has offered him the kitchenless efficiency above the store and an under-the-table stipend of two hundred bucks a week. He took the gig and now waits with faint hope that one of the more clueless start-up conservation companies will call re: the impressive resume he submitted.

"Hey, tiny. I'm trying to show you something here." Dave snaps his fingers so close to Eagle's face that he swears the blade of white overgrowth on Dave's thumbnail grazes his nose. He checks the tip of his nose for blood or the catch of a cut. Underneath the double-bridge of Dave's glasses, he has a vicious unibrow that makes him appear as though he is always scowling, and Eagle wonders if his current expression is an actual scowl.

"Yeah, yeah," Eagle says. He hooks his index finger through the ring crowded with keys that Dave has set on the counter.

"Copies of the keys to the chairlifts and motorized scooters, not that you'll need them. If someone has a question, come get me from the office. Don't want to lose any sales because you don't know what the hell is going on." He shoves a stack of four-color product catalogs into Eagle's hands. "Some light reading."

On the cover an old man and woman race down the street as their fat grandchildren on bicycles pedal after them. Eagle wonders if it is possible to get these scooters rolling that fast, fast enough to outrun a pair of doughy kids eating their way into childhood diabetes. He decides against asking Dave questions for fear of setting him off. Dave has already launched into a tirade once, earlier in the day when Eagle showed up to introduce himself as his boss's nephew and Med Mart's new sales associate. The initial meltdown consisted of Dave pacing little circles around the 800-square-foot showroom and muttering, "If you even, if you even," a rather vague threat Eagle took to mean, "Don't you even fuck this job up for me or I'll end you." Dave does not finish his sentences and this intensifies his menacing qualities.

Dave jabs Eagle's upper arm with the Easton and aims the bat toward the double doors that exit the store. "Outside. I'll show you how we lock up."

Eagle pulls one of the glass doors and it creaks and scrapes the frame's floor-plate as it opens. The difficulty of opening Med Mart's door seems like a quality unsuited to the store's aged customers. So too seem the wads of chewing gum and cigarette butts and Burger King sandwich wrappers, typical city-street trash, littering the front walk, which Dave never sweeps. The parking situation is equally unappealing, with the front curb painted bright red to indicate a tow-away zone.

Dave walks over to a gate retracted against Med Mart's eastern wall and drags it out a few feet to show Eagle the steel diamonds that protect the store from nighttime burglaries. "This is the only defense against an all out break-in. I have three Master Locks in the storeroom to lock this baby up." Dave tells Eagle he puts three locks on everything before Eagle can point out the uniform security measure. "Don't get lazy and use one or two. Those fuckers have no problems breaking one lock."

Dave jabs Eagle with the Easton a second time, probably to make sure he has Eagle's complete and undivided attention, so he nods to reassure Dave, even though he is thinking about his bum ankle and how it has begun to throb again. The ankle is another reminder of recent failures in cheap affairs, the injury the result of a not-so-erotic encounter with his bicycle mechanic friend and a semi-professional dominatrix in San Francisco. After the incident, Eagle's last buddy willing to drink six pints of double IPA and follow him into the backrooms of the City wouldn't return his phone calls. Eagle lost his sublet, and couldn't manage one more call to beg for a couch to crash on.

"Now, I understand you're staying upstairs for a while. I expect you to keep an eye on the place, even when you're sleeping. They're always hurling rocks through the front windows." He taps the bat against the window where a rock has created a crater in the tinted glass.

Eagle again nods and nods, even as his gaze drifts past Dave and down the street to the Vietnamese market where Dave buys his sugar cane. He wonders if they sell booze strong enough for him to drink himself to sleep so he can ignore the ankle's throb and the rocks crashing through showroom windows.

———

The East Bay is on fire. The blonde grass on the ridges burns to black, and the smoke rolls down the hills. Tonight is a rare night in Oakland, one of the few each year when the Pacific fog does not hang over the streets, and people must sleep with their windows pulled open. The suburban folks in the 680 corridor have probably stoked up their air conditioners. The rising temperature of the building forces Eagle to slide open the few windows in the efficiency and sit in his living room/bedroom and breathe the ash-laden air of the many grass fires in the hills. His uncle did not equip the efficiency with any kind of air conditioner, so he sits shirtless on a folding chair and drinks down the twelve-pack of Tecate he bought at the Vietnamese market. The owner welcomed him to the neighborhood with a handshake and two free limes to accompany the cans of beer, bag of rice, and Morton salt he purchased. The owner is one of the few good people Eagle has encountered in a city; he prefers the environmentalists he worked alongside in the field, friends he has lost. Even surrounded by all the denizens of Oakland, he feels more isolated than he did living alone in a stone cabin on Mount Rainier.

The rice boils the lid off the pot, so he drags the pot off the camping stove and onto a towel on the hardwood. He leaves it to sit and will not eat the rice after all because it'll only fill his belly with starch and weaken the nice buzz he has going. The tingle of intoxication begins and his ankle has numbed, even if still turgid with fluid. He cracks open another Tecate and squeezes a wedge of lime into the can's mouth and shakes some salt over the lip. He catches the foam and drinks down a quarter of the can.

Eagle and his worthless, uninsured ankle stumble down the stairs and into Med Mart's showroom, twelve in tow. He makes his way through the boxes of hospital gowns and wound-care products and adult diapers. The storeroom reeks of factory-fresh vinyl from the cases of diabetic shoes stacked high along the staircase. Dave has assigned him the unpleasant task of inventorying the shoes after the company's sales rep came into the store and threw a minor shit-fit when Dave failed to provide sales figures. Although an ancient Dell desktop with a dial-up connection purrs in the showroom, Med Mart has no inventory system and all products are instead labeled with little orange tags spit out of an old-school price gun.

Eagle told Dave he would get a head start on the shoes, but now decides against it in favor of lounging on one of the chairs with a sample seat cushion along the showroom's front windows. He polishes off the can of Tecate and opens another and forgoes the lime and salt that he's grown so fond of. The night traffic of Oakland— salvaged Civics and Cadillacs and Crown Vics—rolls past, loose exhaust systems rattling over the hum of the Dell. He catches a glimpse of himself in the front window and sees that he is looking more and more like his father, deep bags underneath his eyes and creases more pronounced, the terrible cliché realized for its truth. His hairline retreats from his face, amplifying his expressions so that he is now unable to hide his true emotions. He should not have let that hack in Redding mow his hair to a length beyond short. The barber had a waddle like a brown bear's belly that shook when he jabbered on about all the high-and-tights he shaved for soldiers in basic training. The haircut cleared the stench from his tangled, almost knotted hair, but in the end only made Eagle look older and sadder and more hopeless.

He still has the ridge of scar from lip to nostril, of course, like a seam of putty no one bothered to sand, the scar that gives him an unintended snarl. He reaches to pat down what is left of his hair, but now realizes the tight lines expose the divot of flesh where the surgeon harvested the pad of skin that became his upper lip. He tried for the pity fuck once, before he'd had it with cities and escaped to the woods. A woman in a bar thumbed the scar and asked what'd happened, so he told her the story of the golden escaped from the puppy mill next to his father's vineyard and his father sending him to fetch the pup so it wouldn't spoil the grapes. How playful the puppy was, even as it bit him. She seemed disappointed by the story and invited him to a cuddle party in the Marina the following weekend, an invitation he turned down after he learned such parties were limited to cuddling, whatever the hell that meant. He sensed she wanted to continue to paw at his scar during this event, perhaps the fulfillment of some benign fetish.

The only real pride he has left is that he succeeded in not begging his father for a small personal loan—not that he could have helped anyway—or for a couch to crash on for a few months. The truth is he can't stomach the sight of his father, festering in his worn-out elegance. Three Augusts ago, the last time Eagle drove out to Livermore Valley to visit him, they got shit-faced on Jack Daniel's and walked through the rows of scorched leaves and shriveled cabernet grapes. Two non-sequential summers of drought nearly ruined his father, his wine company unable to complete the modern bottling facility he'd worked toward for years. The facility sat roofless, the stonework of the walls spotty and unfinished—a gigantic, humiliating mess that told tasters to stay away. Even tourists from Nebraska wouldn't stop. His father shut down the tasting room and started a consulting firm, which everyone in the business knows is just another way of saying I am unemployed and flat broke.

His mother recently offered her analysis of the graceless arc of

Eagle's life, that it is in close alignment with his father's. He did break down and phone her for money after a man with cheap loafers reclaimed his Vibe, but she said loaning him any money would be a poor investment. His mother has no money of her own, actually, and instead ran off with a man she described as a silver fox, a man who directed medium-budget action films that aired exclusively on SpikeTV and possessed an unimpressive viewership of unemployable meatheads and college athletes. But she was thrilled to be away from the vineyard and its sudden collapse, thrilled to have swapped a quiet glass of cabernet for multiple martinis, a crowded ranch for a gated mansion off Mulholland.

Each time a clunker cruises past Med Mart and the muffler rattles he is reminded of his father in his shaky BMW convertible from the Reagan era, driving through the Livermore Valley to visit other vineyards and push his consulting services. The thought of the sad kit, his father divorced, face sagged, designer suit pilled and worn at the wallet pocket and elbows, causes him to wince and set his beer down on the commode beside him. He starts back upstairs, back to the air mattress in the efficiency. He works at a medical supply store for below minimum wage, but will not become the kind of drunk who sits around alone and duplicates the path of a broken father.

———

Eagle does not understand why the woman sitting next to him is dressed up like a skunk. Even though she has bought him two and a half beers—he counts the double IPA as a half beer because the bartender poured half foam—he still does not know. He does know that her name is Posy, or Po for short, and that she has cobbled together a career as both a yoga instructor and a physical therapist. But in the course of their conversation she has raised several questions about her childhood in a Santa Barbara work commune that go unanswered.

Tonight he is sporting an aircast again, the support device necessary for this little trip to downtown Berkeley. The aircast is a
reminder of his brief, particularly violent reunion with Sage, a
woman who never much cared for him, and never cared enough to
ask about the scar, which was fine by him. He felt the scar was often
a deal breaker with women, especially the vain women he tended
to gravitate toward, and they always seemed to demand some kind
of explanation. But not Sage. Instead, she took out the stress of her
sixty-hour-a-week gig at corporate Gap on him. She threw a lamp
at him one night and he wrenched the ankle while hitting the
hardwood.

And so, here he is, drinking beers in a brewpub crowded with
underage college students and Berkeley hipsters. He knows he is
older than most of them—save for Po—but not so old that he
should not have been carded, or so he thought. When he presented
his ID to the kid at the door, the kid held up his hand and said, "No
problem, sir."

He has been away from Berkeley and Oakland for some time, so
he has spent three evenings down in the better light of the Med Mart
showroom studying the AC Transit route map and schedule so he'll
know when to quit and be able to find his way home without a
terrible walk no matter where he has strayed. Even so, he spaced
and AC Transit dumped him somewhere on Shattuck in the
Gourmet Ghetto and he had to hoof it six blocks back to the brewpub where he hoped to hear some live tunes, down a few real beers,
and find a decent, one-time sexual partner. Instead, he is allowing
Po to buy drinks while he calculates the likelihood of her actually
accompanying him back to Med Mart. He can hardly talk over the
guitar screeches of a bunch of Berkeley dropouts with a Radiohead
complex, but his forced silence is perhaps for the best because he
has lost touch after being in the woods for so damn long.

Po grabs the bartender by the shirtsleeve and orders another round and again refuses his money. He allows her to buy the round, though for the first time in a while he has a few crumpled bills in his pocket. At the end of the day, Dave handed him a pathetic bonus after he sold a discontinued chairlift to some asshole from Albany who'd grown tired of driving over to Montclair to help his mother-in-law up the steep stairs of her home. But Po seems happy to pay and for the third or fourth time expresses her sorrow for his unfortunate ankle situation, especially with him being uninsured and all. She encourages him to take one of her yoga classes at the granola pharmacy on Shattuck when he's well enough and he says yeah, yeah, sounds great. He throws back the splash of beer in the pint glass because he has nothing left to say and must soon come up with a scheme to get a free ride back to Med Mart, at the very least.

The wall clock reads midnight and he has missed the last bus back to the store, so he decides to broach the subject, but Po cuts him off before he can begin. "I lied to you," she says. "I don't live in Berkeley. I'm from San Jose." She stares deep into the amber of her glass as if guilty.

"I don't see why that matters. Listen, is there a chance you can give me a ride back to my place?"

She says sure and they both exit before the bartender can bring their miserable pours. Out on the street, he finally asks her why the hell she's dressed like a skunk, and she says something about a library reading at a local elementary school where her friend teaches. She offers her hand and instead of grabbing it he thinks of the shitty place she will deliver him to. He can't imagine doing anything other than drink with all the mannequins and posters of people very much satisfied with their work scrubs looking down at him. He knows this much: he won't allow her to follow him upstairs to the air mattress because he does not want anyone knowing how he sleeps each night, with poisonous spiders rappelling down to attack him. He does not want anyone to know how each morning he wakes pocked with little red bumps that grow in redness and diameter no matter how vigorously he scrubs in the shower. Dave's office is a possible landing spot, eventually, if he can figure out how to pick all the locks. Dave has all but conceded sales duty to him and he rarely sees Dave during store hours. He suspects Dave has stashed a twin mattress or large wingback in the office for extended naps.

Po shows him to the car, which is not the sedan he expected, but a dated Dodge minivan, iced-mint paint and spotted with patches of rust along the lower panels. The bottom half of the Montana license plate is curled from an attempted theft. He begins to climb into the passenger seat, but stops to brush the Goldfish cracker crumbs off the fabric. He suspected that she might have been bull-shitting him all along, that she was married after all. Po apologizes— he's not sure for what—and he takes his seat and buckles in and says one of his weird, agnostic prayers asking that her husband not lurk somewhere nearby. As she puts the minivan into drive, he looks through the finger smudges on the window and watches a group of college kids pile into a comfortable cab.

"It has been hard finding people who are into the lifestyle, you know," Po says.

He glances in her direction and says, "What lifestyle?" Of course, he knows damn well what she means.

"Oh, I thought—never mind." She falls quiet and places her hands ten and two and accelerates a few miles per hour.

He won't direct her to the store, but to a house on a side street a few blocks away. The efficiency grows stuffy at night and so he has started to walk around his new neighborhood, if he can call it that. Three blocks down Telegraph, he found a paint-stripped ranch with a sickly pine in the front yard, its needles dropped onto the dirt. The leaning pine looked as though its shallow roots would give at any moment, and the owner of the house would have a serious tree removal project. Eagle tried to learn the trade of sustainable harvesting one year by joining the crew of Duke Kane, a legendary sawyer in New England. Duke was less lumberjack and more Cambridge chess player, a tree scholar. He trimmed his beard to shape and kept a thin scarf wrapped tight around his neck. Eagle spent the year trailering Duke's mobile sawmill as the crew chased blow-downs and retrieved beachcombed firs as far as Maine. They'd located an Eastern white pine in the fall, and milled the tree for trail-bridge planking. After the year was up, he begged Duke to keep him on, but Duke said he just couldn't mill worth a damn, he had become a liability, and sent him on his way.

He asks Po to turn off Telegraph. "Yes, right here. The house with the old pine. That's where I live."

———

After Eagle's second week at Med Mart, Dave gives him a promotion of sorts, an event that Dave considers a promotion at least: he invites Eagle into the office. Eagle steps in. Dave takes up the glass pot from the office coffee maker and pours a cup in his MEDI COMPRESSION THERAPY mug. Eagle pretends to sip the coffee, but doesn't let it anywhere near his lips because the surface heat of the mug is roughly equivalent to that of pottery straight out of a kiln and would scald and blister his flesh upon contact. Dave then hands him a faded polo shirt with the Med Mart logo custom-embroidered on the left breast and says, "I think you're ready for this. I want you to start wearing it. You know, to look more professional."

Eagle unfolds it and holds it up in front of him and feigns excitement over this second-hand shirt with white deodorant crust formed on each armpit. Despite its grotesque condition, he will wear the shirt because he doesn't want to wear Dickies work shirts with logos of conservation companies anymore, reminders of the life he had and ruined. He has sent out two dozen resumes in the last three days alone, none of which have yielded so much as a polite acknowledgement. He thanks Dave and refolds the shirt and places it on some boxes filled with arm slings.

"No problem-o," Dave says between licks off today's sugar cane. He works the cane for a minute, then takes a few swallows of the nuclear coffee. For the first time, Dave smiles at Eagle and he gets a good look at Dave's crumbling grill of cracked and coffee-stained teeth. Dave wipes his brow with a stray diabetic sock from his desk and Eagle wants to ask him if he has ever been married or the year of his last date.

"Well, hey. You're just standing in the doorway. Come on in and I'll show you around." He pulls the gold cord on a small lawyer's lamp and the faint light illuminates the collection of antique weapons Eagle had failed to notice. Before he can comment on the swords and knives and bayonets, Dave says, "Nice little collection, huh? Thought you'd be interested."

Eagle starts to say that he has never much cared for knives, but stops because Dave has been kind enough to allow him into the secret world of medical market offices and vintage weaponry. Dave removes a long, Civil War–era bayonet from the wall and hands it to Eagle, just as he handed him the Easton.

"This one isn't for self-defense. Just for show. Don't even have the musket that goes with it." He then trades the bayonet for a more contemporary combat knife, a serious affair with a hyper-serrated back. "Those ridges tear out the victim's guts when you pull the knife out." He takes the knife back and sheathes it and hangs it back on the wall. "Hope those fuckers think about that before they come into my store again."

Eagle doesn't ask what happened before he took the job at Med Mart, but hopes there is no next time. Dave's taunting is a pretty big invitation to robbery motivated by spite and by now he has learned that some of the locals, possible gang members, do not much care for Dave. He learned this from some underage kids after buying beer for them at the Vietnamese grocery store. They offered him twenty bucks, but he refused after he remembered what it was like when he was in that situation. They like Eagle, and promised not to vandalize the store, though last week he found several tags on the back wall of Med Mart, which Dave made him cover up with the blue paint he keeps in the storeroom for such purposes.

Eagle excuses himself from the office and walks to the telephone in the showroom. He dials his uncle's number. His uncle has said not to call except in an emergency, but he must tell his uncle about the lunatic who is managing his investment. His Aunt Linda answers. In a hushed voice Eagle asks to speak with his uncle, but she says he is out of town and will not return until next week. He decides against leaving a message for his uncle because his Aunt Linda has twice been hospitalized after severe panic attacks. She asks if Eagle is well and he says, yes, yes, couldn't be better. "I'm learning a lot from Dave," he says for good measure.

So he now imagines himself in the pitted-out Med Mart shirt, Easton bat readied in hand, with Dave beside him waving the combat knife and the robbers with firearms raised and demanding Dave open the safe so they can remove the contents and slip back into the Oakland streets. They kick Dave and him to the shag carpet of the showroom, bind their hands and feet together with duct tape. He imagines describing the situation to apathetic detectives and to local news reporters afterward. There he is with the Med Mart shirt and his scar, snarling at the general public as they digest their dinners. He will need to be ready. Tonight he will bring the Easton up to the efficiency and take practice swings in the dark.

——

Po's name is not Po, as it would turn out, but Amy. She tells him this when she corners him near the restroom payphone in the brewpub. Against his better judgment, which he does not really possess, he returned to the pub with the latest cash transfusion from his uncle. He seems to be what people call lonely. The twelver of Tecate he drinks in the showroom each night convinces him that the tingle in his forearms is anxiety, anxiety perhaps caused by isolation. He walks around the neighborhood with greater frequency, but never explores the areas beyond the house with the pine tree unless he walks to the pub in Berkeley. He often visits the pine, where he stands at the chain-link fence and considers entering the yard to pay the tree a visit. But then the owner came outside last night—a fat, messy man with a bathrobe that did little to conceal his body—and told Eagle to move along. "You're scaring my kid," he said.

And so he has been stupid enough to return to the brewpub. Po, or Amy, offers to buy him a drink, but he says no way, no way. He has been down this road with her once now and does not want married women who may or may not live the "lifestyle" pawing at his body as they transport him home in their shaky minivan. Most sane adults wouldn't consider Eagle a realistic possibility for her anyway; she shouldn't get involved with him because he lives above the place where he works, has teeth that are more and more looking like Dave's, and is the only person in Berkeley who would go to a bar while wearing a new-old pitted-out Med Mart shirt without trying to be ironic. Dave has also requested that he not welcome guests into the store or the efficiency because he believes most people in Berkeley and Oakland have a genuine interest in history and antique weapons. Dave fears his collection is known to certain members of the community and might be the target of future burglaries, which raises questions about why he chooses to keep his collection locked up in the office and not somewhere more reasonable, like his own home.

Po wraps her hands around her drink and says, "I can tell I make you uncomfortable." And she's right. He doesn't understand married people. In the ten years since high school graduation, many of his friends have fallen victim to marriage, which has made most of them broke, overweight, and disappointed. And though he is broke and disappointed with his current share in life, he is at least not overweight. In fact, despite his ankle's deterioration he now walks the three miles to and from the bars in Berkeley just so he will not end up bloated from unrestrained IPA consumption.

He is paranoid that Po's husband lurks somewhere nearby. He surveys the pool tables and watches the men who appear to be alone. Several middle-aged men with receding hairlines—the type of people he has never seen here before—lean against the far wall and twirl pool cues and gnaw at their upper lips as they study the tables. Any one of them could be Po's husband. He wonders for a moment if he is dealing with another animal altogether: a couple from Montana who gets in good with mellow folks in Berkeley and Oakland so that they can beat and rob them. But perhaps the creepy vibe originates in Po's commitment to the "lifestyle." He does not know much about people active in the "lifestyle," really. His knowledge is limited to the handful of former acquaintances who spent their Saturday afternoons crafting and responding to Craigslist ads that sought singles who enjoyed dressing up like stuffed animals and such. He once knew a barista in the city who really got off on this sort of thing, though the guy had several stories that involved dark warehouses in South City, wall-climbing equipment, and workaholic spouses who were not, as it turned out, all that cool with what happened with their husband or wife. No matter how desperate Eagle gets, he does not want end up hiding in the store with Easton in hand while some pissed-off guy screams at him through the gate and windows.

Po hands him a business card and he does not look at it. He slips it into his back pocket and plans to discard it in one of the trashcans outside the brewpub. She encourages him to call her. "You seem lonely. I think we can help each other."

Over curses from men near the pool table, he thanks her for the ride a few weeks ago, but must go before his ankle swells to the point of uselessness.

—

Dave finds the job-posting Eagle had been checking out the previous night. He rarely comes into work early, but today he found Eagle asleep, reclined on one of the lift chairs in the showroom and covered in stale Tecate from the evening before, and the job posted on New Wilderness Conservation's website pulled up on the humming Dell's screen.

"You are dishonest," he says. He clicks around the desktop, picks up the mouse, shakes it, and calls it a piece of shit. The mouse is a piece of shit, one of the stock roller ball deals that clogs with crumbs and stalls when you're navigating a webpage. The problem is compounded by Dave's general incompetence with electronics. He doesn't use the Dell often, so Eagle used it for non–Med Mart purposes without much anxiety, never expecting him to discover the automated response from the human resources department at New Wilderness Conservation. The job is pathetic anyway, a glorified map-printer, but Eagle has taken to spending his late evenings drinking a case of Tecate and responding to terrible jobs with a fake name and resume. In a week's time, the inbox for the e-mail address he created in support of this effort is packed with pornographic spam messages, which he has not bothered to delete.

"You are a sick fuck," Dave says, not understanding. Eagle agrees with this statement on some level though. Even with the weapons stockpile Dave maintains in the office, Eagle is still more fucked in the head. He has spent the last six years of his life living in and out of the wilderness, often living alone in a tent in a pine forest that needs a small trail bridge repaired. While Dave has wasted much of his life talking old folks into home healthcare products they don't need and can't afford, Eagle wasted much of his early life talking bears and coyotes and mountain lions out of stalking and skinning him alive as he went about his work assessing trails.

"Sick. Just sick," Dave says again. He unplugs the computer and reaches underneath the counter for the Easton. Now Dave will kill him, this much is sure. Dave grips the bat's midsection and slaps the end against his palm. "You, friend," he starts, "are not long for Med Mart." He twirls the Easton as if it is a baton. Eagle sits up in the lift chair and prepares for impact. His ankle remains swollen from the long trek back to the store after his last night of drinking at the brew-pub in Berkeley. This is how it will end for him: clocked in the head with an aluminum Easton while inside his uncle's medical supply store on Telegraph in Oakland. He is somewhat relieved, now knowing.

Dave raises the bat's tip at him and says, "Now, I am going to lock myself in the office so I can call that bat-shit crazy uncle of yours. And I'm going to tell him what a sicko you are and that I want you out of my store."

"No problem-o," Eagle says with his best attempt at Dave's voice. He stands and slips off the Med Mart shirt and folds it up and hands it to Dave. "I won't need this anymore."

Dave pulls the shirt out of his hands and retreats to the office, Easton tucked under his left arm. Eagle stands there bare-chested for a moment, then follows Dave to the storeroom to lounge on boxes while Dave places the awkward call to his uncle. His uncle will not defend him, this much he knows. He has twice failed to be a productive employee at one of his uncle's train-wreck business ventures. The first time was in high school, when he worked at his uncle's smog check station in Tracy and simply passed vehicles without bothering to connect them to the machine. This was hot, dirty work that paid shit and required him to don a tight-fitting one-piece mechanic's suit, but it was also the lousy job that later encouraged him to find something well-paying and outdoors.

Through Dave's office door, Eagle can hear him speak to his uncle. "Well, you better have him out of here soon . . . Yes, there were photographs. Sick stuff. Really sick." Eagle reclines on a recent shipment of compression garments and listens to Dave berate his uncle who, despite his rather serious demeanor, is known to avoid conflict. Eagle imagines Dave calling Med Mart after hours later tonight to harass him further and suggest Eagle seek employment elsewhere not because he has received dirty e-mails on Med Mart's Dell, but because he has betrayed Dave's trust by sending resumes to other potential employers.

Eagle shoves his hands into his pockets in search of stray singles he can put toward dinner. Dave throws something against the wall, probably the phone. Dave will stay fortified inside his office for the remainder of the afternoon, unless he decides to remove Eagle from Med Mart himself. Inside his pocket, Eagle finds a ratty ten and Po's bent-up business card. He will be able to throw himself one hell of a going away party.

—

Po is on her way over to Med Mart, so he decides to make one last pot of rice on the camping stove before her arrival. When he called, a child in the background talked over her and he wonders if calling her was a good idea after all. "One minute," she said. "I have to go outside." He tried to give her an out, said it sounds like this is a bad time, but she insisted on coming over. "Give me an hour."

His hi-tech camping stove boils a liter of water in just four minutes, so he will be able to eat the last cup of rice in his efficiency. In the field, he often needed quick fuel after a day of sawing trees off trails or boating pine boards across still ponds. He goes to fire up the butane burner, but the canister is cashed. The stove makes a slight hissing noise as the last fuel drains. He checks his pack for one of the many spare canisters he poached from the conservation company's stock-house, but he is already out. He is slowly losing the signs of ever having worked in conservation. After six years, he imagined he'd become one of those industry folks who could no longer stay inside buildings or cook meals in civilian kitchens. When he first returned to the Bay Area, he refused to sleep in a building, thought he could not, and instead pitched his half-dome in friends' yards. But he has been sleeping inside the efficiency for almost four weeks now without even noticing.

He collapses the stove and stuffs it inside his pack and clips the pack closed. The gear inside is not properly distributed, but he heaves it onto his back anyway. He takes a few steps and nearly topples over; he hasn't carried a pack in almost two months and his body is not accustomed to the extra weight.

The showroom lights are still on, but he doesn't bother to turn them off. If Po and her husband are in fact burglars or whatever, he wants to make Med Mart an easy job, with plenty of light and no locks on the back door. He would pick the locks on Dave's office, where the cash is stored, for them, but even after several Tecate-soaked nights he still cannot figure out how to release them. Dave has accused him of attempting to break into the office twice now, citing the scuffmarks on the Master Locks' metal, and replaced the locks with new, more severe ones.

Telegraph is quiet for a Thursday. A retired squad car rolls past him, its rear shocks blown, and the bumper taps the ground with each road-seam. One more stroll around the neighborhood is in order before he catches BART back to the City to patch things up with Chase and find a couch to crash on for a few weeks.

He walks past the boarded up shops, past the Vietnamese market, and toward the street with the pine. The owner of the market waves at him through the bars on his store's windows and returns to denying a liquor-sale to a group of obvious minors. Eagle would have bought the kids booze had he been visiting the store for his own because he supports the store owner's business. No one makes it on Telegraph, but the man's still here after twenty-five years.

He turns the corner on the side street and sees the pine ahead, the trunk gone horizontal and fallen over the chain-link fence. Those shallow roots wouldn't have held much longer, and it looks as though a landscaping crew has felled the tree. The trunk extends halfway into the street, suggesting a general incompetence on the part of the crew. The homeowner has taped a sign to the trunk with a polite note: PLEASE EXCUSE MY TREE.

Eagle tears the sign off the pine and wads it into a ball. He sits on the curb's edge and tosses the note toward a city trashcan across the street, but misses. He never was any good at traditional sports like basketball.

The house's front door opens and the owner, wearing nothing but a pair of revealing boxer shorts, steps outside. "Excuse me, buddy," he says. "What did I tell you about standing there looking at my house?"

"Sorry," Eagle says. He stands and brushes pine shavings off his jeans.

"Yeah, move along." The man waves his arm, his sack of bicep fat swinging with emphasis.

"Sure." Eagle starts to move down the street, but stops. He scoops up a fistful of the pine's meal in the gutter and brings it close to his face. "Just a minute," he says, and waits for the scent of forest to rise to him.

Wild Horse

 arrive home to find Adam striking the townhouse's mailbox with an aluminum bat. Our neighbor Eileen is sitting in a bent lawn chair in the snow with a mildewed comforter draped over her shoulders. She pulls on her Pall Mall and cheers for my son as he pummels our mailbox. Bear wags his tail and barks every time Adam takes a swing. The mailbox begins to break away from the building, but that isn't enough to persuade me to shout at him from the parking lot. I've just gotten off my shift at the prison, and Adam has more fight in him right now.

By the time I reach Adam, he has beat the mailbox off the building and it has fallen into the ratty boxwoods beside our door. His coat has gone missing. He tucks his arms inside the sleeves of his T-shirt. Bear trots over to us and tries to jump up on my chest, but I tell him to stay down. I set my hand on Adam's shoulder.

"Easy now," I say. A few pieces of junk mail litter the front stoop of our townhouse.

Adam doesn't acknowledge me. He drops the bat and takes off down the sidewalk toward the complex's playground. If I give chase, he will just evade me and disappear into the wilds of the Sleepy Hollow trailer park next door. I watch him as he works his way into one of the playground's small tunnels where he often hides and stares at the wild horses pacing in the sanctuary in the distance. Some nights he will stay out there for two, three hours, long after the sun has lowered behind the Sierra. I watch over him from the window above the kitchen's range while I heat a frozen dinner and Bear sleeps at my feet.

My wife hasn't sent Adam a letter in months. A year ago, she skipped town with a long-haul trucker ten years her junior, leaving Adam in my care. She was good about sending him letters about her travels. Maybe she also felt some level of obligation to tell me her whereabouts. The letters mostly contained irrelevant details of her trip, as she liked to call it. She won a c-note playing penny slots in Elko, spent an afternoon glow bowling in Salt Lake City, got violently ill from a gas station hot dog in Rock Springs. A rather aggressive ostrich resided at a private zoo outside Salina. Oklahoma City had an expansive dance hall where a group of cowboys taught her how to two-step. Her last letter arrived a month later, just after the first snowfall here on the eastern Sierra slope. The letter was postmarked Coos Bay, but didn't include a return address. *You won't hear from Mom for a while,* she wrote. I pretended I hadn't read the letter and asked Adam how his mother was getting along. Our potpies rotated in the microwave. He put on his coat and Red Wings and headed out the door without saying anything.

"That boy of yours has energy," Eileen says. She burns another crater in the chair's arm with her cigarette and tosses the butt into the snow bank along the walk. Bear nuzzles against her leg, and she plays with the tips of his soft ears. "Kid has been beating on that mailbox since he got home from school."

"What happened to his coat?" I say.

"Lost it."

I collect the mail before the wind blows it across the complex's quad and stand shuffling through the envelopes to see if Linda has written Adam, though I know she hasn't.

"Don't tell Benny," I say to Eileen. "He gets upset about things like this. I can hang it back up myself."

She sips jug wine from the Diamond Mountain Casino travel mug she always keeps close to her. "Oh, Breaker. You need to tell me what's in it for poor old Eileen," she says.

"I'll give you a raise to ten an hour to watch over Adam," I say.

She takes another swig of wine and considers my offer. Bear lets out a low woof when she stops playing with his ears. When Linda left, I turned to Eileen to watch Adam after the bus drops him off. Most nights I return home to find Adam shooting hoops in the moonlight. Eileen will tell Benny to toss some Ice Melt on the slick court, then retire to my townhouse to pick the lock on the small liquor cabinet where I keep my bourbon. I often find her passed out on the recliner in the family room, illuminated by the glow of the evening news on television.

Eileen raises her thumb toward the sky. "Eileen has expenses."

"Fifteen."

"So generous. Corrections must pay well."

The prison doesn't. The small junior college where I served as athletic director experienced sweeping budget cuts in the fall, and the board reduced my position to half time and eliminated my benefits. I started teaching remedial reading to inmates in the prison's continuing education center for extra money, though I haven't been in a classroom since well before Adam was born. I am struggling to hide my incompetence from the educational administrator. He is a fair and kind man, but has begun encouraging me to return to coaching football at the high school next fall, where I have a standing offer to coordinate the struggling offense.

"I hope you know he's a good kid," Eileen says. She glances up at me. Her eyes have yellowed, the life drained out of them long ago. "He's going to make it, that one. He'll be just fine when his mother returns."

"I know," I lie. A few months ago, Adam's teacher reported that he had started carving deep grooves into the lip of his desk and wouldn't speak to other kids. Soon after, the principal expelled Adam from the after-school program when he choked another boy. The boy had made a passing remark about the state of the athletic department at the college. When I arrived to pick up Adam, the boy's mother was evaluating the spots of bruise on her son's neck. I apologized, but knew Adam would be marked until he graduated or abandoned Susanville for Portland or San Francisco.

Adam has always gravitated toward Linda's Southern Californian impulsiveness and shunned my Midwestern reserve. I spent my adolescence hurling my body into other kids on the muddy football fields of Milwaukee while Linda wandered the boardwalk and talked revolutions with radicals in Venice Beach. In high school I brooded over athletic scholarships and a collapsing knee. Linda skipped school to get stoned and surf until the sun fell over the Pacific.

"You know," Eileen says. "This town used to be a good place to grow up. We'd walk down to the river and catch trout. We'd walk to the movie theaters uptown. The sawmill's whistle would go off at the end of every shift. We could rely on things like that whistle."

Eileen likes to lament the fall of the sawmill and blame the prisons for the downward course of her life. Half of the town's population consists of inmates at High Desert State Prison. The other half is made up of correctional officers and ex-mill employees and people waiting for someone on the inside to get paroled. Most residents scrape by with part-time work at a motel or IGA or the college between contracts at the military depot an hour away.

I suspect Eileen is living in Susanville while she waits for someone on the inside. She doesn't seem to know anyone around town beyond her transient daughter who stops by the townhouse to do a load of laundry and smoke a bowl on the playground. Eileen never questions her daughter and the shirtless men with face tattoos she brings around. Eileen just offers them a frozen pizza and a place to rest their heads for the night. I admit to listening to their conversations through the wall.

"Sometimes I think this town will get back to what it was," Eileen says. She pulls the comforter tighter around her body. "We're going to be just fine."

I pat Bear on the back and motion for him to go inside. I call for Adam. He crawls out of the tube, but keeps his back to me. He makes a snowball and rifles it at the basketball hoop. It explodes against the backboard.

———

When Adam falls asleep on the sofa, I take a bottle of Deschutes out of the fridge and rouse Bear and nudge him outside. He stumbles out the door and sniffs the snow bank along the walk. I use the door's strike-plate to pop the cap off the bottle, a trick my dad taught me the afternoon he handed me my first Miller. We'd been cutting flagstone for a patio he was laying for a wealthy couple who lived near Lake Michigan. The bottle's cool sweat felt right against my dust-chalked hands. We stood in the couple's garage and drank in silence until we emptied the bottles. I often think of leaving Susanville to find stable work in a city like Stockton or Fresno, a city where I can afford a house with a garage, a place where I can teach my son the intrinsic satisfaction of the small trades, where I can offer him his first bottle of Pabst.

The evening is cold and still, the moon bright over the valley. It is the first night in weeks we haven't had a rush of low clouds over the mountains. Bear and I cut through the clearing behind the complex of townhouses to the iced-over pond where Bear likes to chase the mule deer come down from the deep snow of the mountains.

Winters in Susanville made Linda stir-crazy and pushed her into the casino and tavern, she claimed. But I often thought it was my workload before I went down to half time—the lost hours spent tracking down prospects who failed to meet the academic requirements to maintain a division one scholarship, the evenings inside the sweaty gymnasiums, the Sundays counseling homesick student-athletes in my office on campus. The hours added up to nothing more than a cut in pay and broken family in a remote mountain town. Could the family have driven her away? Had she decided to leave years ago, in the bathroom of our dumpy studio apartment in Reno as she held the pregnancy test? She was twenty. I was twenty-eight. We were still trying to find our direction, our way. I was working long days for a consulting firm that tracked statistics for college coaches. She called me into the bathroom one morning, and I found her sitting on the toilet holding the drug-store pregnancy test. "I'm too young," she said, flipping the test into the wastebasket.

Linda hadn't wanted to move to Susanville and resisted the idea of embedding herself in the community. "We don't fit in here," she said. I kept telling myself she'd adjust, that anyone could adjust to this place.

I take Bear past the lone trailer home in the clearing and toward the reservoir. The light of a television bounces off the drapes, and the silhouette of someone inside crosses the window. The trailer's door opens, and a flannel-clad drunkard steps onto the makeshift porch. He slurs something at us, but he's too far for me to hear. Bear barks and goes to drive the man away, but I wrangle him by the collar and move him along. The locals turn at night. Their drink brings out a streak of country-mean unkind to imports like myself. This is the time of night you'll see old pickups lurching down Main, bald Goodyears crossing double-yellows. You'll see townies pouring out of the bowling alley's bar at close, cracking knuckles, chasing traveling salesmen and state auditors into the parking lot. I worry about raising Adam in a choked-off place like this, that I don't take him down to Reno or San Francisco enough, that one day he may catch on with a group of drifters and disappear into the wilds of Eastern Oregon.

I saw the same tendency in Linda. Mid-conversation, she would stand, slip on her yachting shoes and withdraw into the night. At first, she wasn't gone more than an hour, but that hour became two and three and then entire days. I would wake Adam, bundle him up, and go out into the cold to search for her. Early on, I found her at the tribal casino outside town, talking to older men over a cigarette and a Lagunitas. Then, I would find her around town— drinking rail whiskey at the tavern uptown, standing out on Main trying to hitchhike to Reno, crashing at rent-controlled apartments full of meth-traffickers and transients.

The last night I saw Linda, I had tracked her down at the Riverbend Inn where she was holed up in a room with the long-haul trucker. She was using again. I knew before the door to their room even opened. I knocked and caught a right hook from the trucker as soon as he opened the door. As I went down, I spotted burnt squares of foil and cashed lighters. I like to remember that I saw Linda as I stumbled to my feet, but I know I only heard her voice from inside the room. She was saying go, get out, go.

I release Bear and stumble over the uneasy terrain of the clearing, try to avoid rolling an ankle on the rocks breaking under the cover of snow. The terrain of Susanville, the valley where the high desert cuts off the dense patches of the Sierra's forest, is always shifting. The uncertainty of the terrain prevents the wild horses in the pasture from attempting to break free. The only thing they can do is walk the fence, look out over the expanse of the sagebrush and juniper.

Bear reaches the pond and sniffs along the contours of the shoreline. He has never had an interest in venturing onto the ice. The threat of the ice giving out reminds me of playing pond hockey in the park as a kid. We'd play close to the shore, so we would stay upright, leg stuck half a foot below, if we punched a skate through the ice. We'd heard the story about the neighborhood kid who'd skated out to the center years before. The ice in the center was thin and gave way when the weight of him passed over it. The police didn't recover his body until morning.

I've often thought about the seconds the boy fall in, what it would be like to hear the ice cracking and pause, knowing you're going under. I imagine the ice breaking on a brisk night when the moon is full and bright and shining down on the pond. I imagine the creak and the ice breaking and the rush of falling. The water taking hold of my body and the fight leaving me. I imagine my last glance upward, seeing the tree-shadows dancing on the surface the moment just before the mind switches off.

—

I'm halfway to the prison when the school calls about Adam. I pull into a shuttered gas station where a man in Carhartt overalls is loading rusty propane tanks into the back of a pickup. He stops and sets down a tank when he sees me. The high desert wind kicks up a swirl of snow and road-trash. He stares me down as cigarette butts and plastic shopping bags blow around him. I take the phone off speaker so I can hear the principal. Her voice cuts in and out, but I catch something about a scuffle and Adam in the nurse's office. His face. The call drops before she can finish.

I turn the car around and get back on the highway towards town. A thick layer of clouds hangs over the Sierra, dumping snow down to the ridgeline just above town. A CalTrans plow drops sand on the road in front of me. I slow behind it and sand pelts my windshield in its wake. We drive through snowed-over stretches of empty land outside town, past the abandoned farm machinery and collapsed barns. The plow's driver keeps it at an even 35. I tap the gas pedal so my Pontiac's alternator doesn't quit. When we reach the city limits, the driver drops the plow's blade and clears the snow spilled into the road. The blade sparks along the gutters of Burger King and Grocery Outlet and Dollar General.

In the school's parking lot I find a single lifted truck parked at an angle occupying the two visitor's spaces. The rest of the lot is crowded with rusty Oldsmobile and Buick sedans. I find a spot cut off by an ice-hardened snow bank and roll the Pontiac up on it.

The community safety officer is pacing in the pick-up circle outside the school. I say hello to him, but he just eyes me. He caught Adam with a book of matches on school property a few months back. The book had the casino's logo printed on it. Adam had found them in the light jacket Linda left behind in the townhouse's front closet.

Inside the office, the administrative assistant starts to greet me, but Mrs. Prchal, the principal, intercepts me.

"I'll walk you to the nurse's office," she says.

We walk through a hallway lined with lockers students have defaced with skateboard company stickers and profanities scratched into the paint. The edges of the lockers are bent out from attempts at vandalism. There aren't any posters encouraging students to join afterschool activities or athletics. The school discourages students from hanging around beyond the final bell.

Mrs. Prchal's eyes are sunken and hollow, the flesh around the sockets gone loose from three decades in a low-performing school system. Her suit is pilled and mended in places where the original threadwork has given out. She has run the school for years and parents believe she is the only person in town capable of maintaining order at a school where children of prisoners and prison guards collide. Her position at the school gained her an invitation to serve on the college's board where she organized the movement to reduce my position as athletic director to half time.

"Your son is a very disruptive child," she says.

"His mother moved away. He's adjusting."

We stop in front of the door to nurse's office. I hear the nurse ask Adam if he needs a new bag of ice. He tells her to leave him alone.

"His teacher isn't a disciplinarian. She believes she can help the troubled ones find their way with compassion." She pauses and looks off into nowhere. "We live in very different times."

I walk into the nurse's office without saying anything. The nurse points to the patient room off to the side and smiles. She's the kind of person residents of the town should see only on television screens, hair professionally styled, clothes tailored to her figure, like Linda during the good years before we moved here.

Adam slouches in a chair, blue icepack over his eye. The fight stretched out the neck of his T-shirt. He doesn't move when I lower myself to a knee and greet him.

"Hey, buddy," I say again. I remove the icepack from his face. A brushstroke of blue colors the skin beneath his eye. When I examine the injury, he clamps his jaw tighter and trembles. His eyes are empty and far off—Linda's eyes. He looks through me.

———

Adam continues to fight after I put him to sleep. I hear him stirring and kicking the walls in his room. He grunts and swipes the reading lamp off his nightstand. The old bed frame creaks as it twists into a new shape. His heels hit the floor and he stomps.

The wind has calmed and heavy snow has begun to fall. Benny is out there with one of his assistants. He drags a bag of Ice Melt around the complex's walks and tosses handfuls of it on the pavement. The complex's handyman is messing around with the snow blower over by the maintenance garage. He has the guard over the blade removed and beats on something in the motor.

I get my coat and pull on my Red Wings. Bear is resting on his side against the door, deep in sleep. His paws twitch. I gently shake him from his dream and tell him to go get Adam. He blinks a few times, flips over, and leaps up the stairs. I go to the basket of unfolded laundry in the family room and fish out a fresh pair of socks and a sweatshirt for Adam. I carry the clothes to the base of the staircase. Adam appears at the top with Bear at his side.

"Let's go for a walk," I say.

"I hate walking," he says.

Bear pays no attention to Adam's protest. He nudges Adam's legs and herds him down the stairs. "Bear!" Adam shouts as he plods downstairs. He stops and wrestles Bear to the floor, but Bear breaks free and playfully nips at his hands.

I hand the sweatshirt and socks to Adam and open the front closet to get his boots and my old Chicago Cubs coat.

"It's snowing," I say, handing him the coat.

He pulls it on and it hangs off his narrow frame. "I hate snow."

"We'll have a snowball fight."

I open the door, and Adam reluctantly steps onto the front stoop. Bear races out the door and tumbles in the snow. He barks and runs circles around us, kicking up snow and ruining the fresh blanket fallen over the quad's lawn. Adam picks up a fistful of snow and fires it at Bear. The snowball bursts on Bear's back, but he just shakes it off.

Eileen is standing in her doorway, smoking. She blows a cloud of smoke into the sky. "That's some shiner you have there, kid," she says to Adam.

"Some dumb kids at school," he says. He lowers his head and pokes his boot's toe into the stoop.

"Hope you got a shot in," she says. She flicks her cigarette onto the walk and retreats into her townhouse.

Bear takes off across the complex's quad and jumps up on the handyman. The guy stops and scratches Bear's ears.

"Where do you go at night?" Adam says to me. He looks right at me for the first time since Linda left us.

"There's a pond across the fields," I say. "I can take you there."

Adam turns toward the darkness of the fields. In the distance, the silhouettes of the horses move through the pasture. The horses are always restless during heavy snowfall. They walk the pasture's fence together, looking for gaps. They look out beyond the fences and see us, then the open stretches of high desert, land like the Nevada wild they used to freely inhabit.

I pat Adam on the shoulder. "Follow me," I say.

We cut through the fresh snowfall and pass the handyman and dead snow blower, the few cars in the parking lot, and walk into the fields. The snow is deep and gives until our boot-soles hit the ground below. Bear sniffs out the trail, catches it, and we follow him through the darkness.

We pass the grove of scrubby pine and the trailer home and row of gutted cars. The trailer casts dim light across the clearing. The trailer's owner stands at the door, watching us as we make our way toward the pond. He cradles a beer can and doesn't wave. When I look away, I fight off images of Linda: Linda holed up in a camper with the trucker, Linda listening to coastal rain slapping the aluminum roof, Linda pulling on a glass pipe, Linda underneath another man.

The owner whistles at us and shouts a warning about trespassing. The boom of his voice startles Adam and Bear, and they take off toward the pond. I give chase, boots punching through the hardened snow and ankles threatening to roll on loose rocks underneath.

Bear stops at the pond's shore. Adam rushes past him and presses on. He doesn't feel the ground underneath his boots change or the slick of the pond's ice. I stomp through snowdrifts and patches of grass, but I'm too late. He's already heading toward the center. I fight through hard coughs and call out to Adam. He doesn't turn back.

ACKNOWLEDGMENTS

I would like to thank Susan Gubernat, Toni Graham, Steve Gutierrez, Brandon Hobson, Mason Hayes, Lisa Lewis, Dinah Cox, Jon Billman, Robert Mayer, Lindsay Wilson, James Brubaker, Jake Williams, Dave Andersen, and Justin Obara.

Many thanks to Nahid Rachlin for selecting my manuscript, Karen Fisk, Carol Betsch, Sally Nichols, and the staff of University of Massachusetts Press, and the Association of Writers & Writing Programs.

Some of these stories, in slightly different forms or with different titles, appeared in the following journals: *Arroyo*, "Wild Horse"; *Southern Indiana Review*, "Gar"; *REAL: Regarding Arts & Letters*, "Temper"; *Heavy Feather Review*, "Alley Cat"; *Confrontation*, "Scrap"; *Midwestern Gothic*, "Gritters"; *PANK*, "Bee inside a Bullet"; *Pilgrimage*, "Lifer"; *Ride: Short Fiction about Bicycles*, "Polo"; *Crossborder*, "Wake"; *Big Fiction*, "Telegraph."